SEVEN
Days in
SAVANNAH

JW AMBROSE

Quantum
Discovery
A LITERARY AGENCY

Seven Days in Savannah
Copyright © 2025 by JW Ambrose

Library of Congress Control Number: 2025900069

ISBN
979-8-89641-032-4 (Paperback)
979-8-89641-033-1 (eBook)
979-8-89641-031-7 (Hardcover)

The characters in this book
are completely fictional. Any
resemblance to anyone living or dead
is purely coincidental.

Table of Contents

ACKNOWLEDGEMENT

I would like to express my deepest gratitude to my wife, Debbie, for her unconditional support and love, which have served as a continual source of strength for me. To my family, thank you for the encouragement and belief in me.

A special thanks to Sara Moore from Quantum Discovery for their outstanding contribution throughout this journey. Your expertise and commitment have helped bring this book to life.

INTRODUCTION

Tristan casually laid the photo album on top of the hope chest while he searched for the old Navy buttons he had promised his grandson. How long it had been since he had browsed in the attic, especially this part of it. There were many memories stored up here; some good and some not so good, but never the less, they were his. The laughter of the children in the yard was plentiful. His daughter and grandson had been more frequent in their visits lately. He guessed it was because he was alone now and they thought he had nothing to do. There it was the old wooden box that held the remnants of his many tours of duty in the navy.

He would never forget the week he visited Savannah. He never thought that those seven days would change his life forever. Julianne, his daughter, reached the top of the steps just as he was closing the lid on the trunk.

"I never realized this stuff was still up here," she said. "The last time we were up here, we cleaned out a lot of boxes that belonged to grandmother." *Tristan's mother had passed away and all of her important and not so important papers had been stored in his attic.*

They made their way down the stairs with the small wooden box. Ryan had been waiting with anticipation looking forward to playing with the buttons. He had been collecting navy memorabilia since his fifth birthday. His fascination with large military ships had done nothing but grown recently. Tristan opened the box, and not only was the buttons there, but there was the locket that he had given to Julia (his wife) the day he left. A crooked smile pursed his lips as the tears welled up in his eyes when he read the note she left him. Just as Julianne was about to speak, Jeffrey, her son, came into the room. She simply gave her dad a soft touch on the hand and a quick wink. She understood more than he thought.

Chapter One

The wind from the Savannah River was brisk as he made his way down the cobblestone street. Although the sidewalks were smoother than the roadway, they were still uneven. The fountain in front of the Pirate's Den restaurant was brightly lit as usual. The flowing water from the jets illuminated the sides of the bronze statue standing guard over the pool. Not too many people were familiar with the story of Captain Jack, the famous pirate who stormed the canal and took all the prisoners whom he was to take to the orient to be sold as slaves. His men would get the workers drunk and they would wake up the next day on board a ship destined for parts unknown, never to be seen again by the locals. The secret underground tunnel that led from the wine cellar in the basement to the docks afforded them the invisibility of dragging the men to their doom and onto the awaiting ships.

He walked up the stairs to the dining room, and after talking to the matre' d his request was honored.

The waitress seated him near the window area, as he requested. The sunsets from this position were breathtaking. This was his second night to visit the restaurant. The beer was cold, and the seafood was very good. He was bound and determined to enjoy his last week of leave time before going on his next tour of duty. The ship that awaited him was anchored out in the harbor and would be leaving shortly, in one more week. Like the captives of long ago, he wondered where his ship would be bound for, as he had not received his orders yet, and wouldn't until he arrived on board. Just as the waiter approached to take his drink order, she appeared out of nowhere. Her fluid motion was captivating. Her mere presence in the room seemed to light up the whole area. Her long black hair danced with every step and her dark eyes mirrored the vibrant reflections of the candles.

Julia Deveraux had lived in Savannah most of her life. The four years she had attended college was her only sabbatical from the city. Her father had been stationed there during the war, and he and her mother met at one of the local gathering spots. They were married shortly thereafter and lived a long and fulfilled life there. Her parents had long since passed away, and she wiled away her days with her writing. She was in the process of writing her third book. The first two had been an instant success. Her agent was pushing for her to finish it quickly, but she just wasn't into it right now. She had visited the lighthouse and watched the sunset more than once this week. As the waiter sat her at her favorite table, she glanced over at Tristan and gave him a smile. Her eyes reflected the soft light of the candles, and he was almost embarrassed that she had caught him taking an extra long look. The evening rays of the sun gleamed off his prematurely gray hair, and the clouds in the background were the perfect setting for the evening. His lobster and steak were scrumptious and the wine was tasty to the pallet. A couple of times during dinner he caught a glimpse of her looking his way. He wondered if she was looking at the sunset or if she was stealing a look at him.

After dinner he casually walked out onto the balcony to finish his drink. The view from the second floor out over the river was breathtaking. The sound of the boats navigating up and down the river blended with the sounds of the people walking up and down the street, meandering in and out of the Shoppe's. There was a peaceful calm about this place, he had traveled all over the world, been in some exotic places, but none as peaceful as this one. The cool evening breeze slightly tussled his hair, and as he turned to go back inside, she stood in the doorway.

"Enjoying the evening?" she asked.

"Very much," he replied. "The scenery is absolutely beautiful!"

She gave him that soft little smile again and decided to play his game. *This guy is pretty smooth, she thought, I probably should watch him.*

"Care for a drink?" he asked.

"I already have two on the way," she said.

"Thought maybe you might be in the mood for another and some conversation." She walked over to the rail and leaned in close to him. She caught a whiff of his cologne and was impressed by his stature. Not too much, just clean and smooth. After the usual small talk, introductions and general information, they found themselves strolling along the river walkway. As they passed the statue of the waving girl, Florence Martus, Tristan asked if her story was true, and she replied that it was. She seemed unusually comfortable with him. He was very easy to talk to. A short time later, they found themselves in the middle of downtown near the parking lot where he had parked his rental. " Care for a guided tour?" she asked.

"My old Chevy is parked just around the corner, and with the top down, the evening air will be soothing and will give better views."

Many thoughts ran through his mind. Here he is with one of the most beautiful women he had ever met, and just had met her a couple of hours ago.

"Sure," he replied. "Just need to make sure you don't have any axes in the trunk."

"I'll dispose of the body properly," she laughed.

With that they took off. As they drove through town, he noticed the beauty of the old antebellum homes. For the next 30 minutes she gave him the quick informational tour of the city. The statues in the parks were exceptionally interesting.

" Ever been to Bonaventure Cemetery?" she asked.

"I don't usually frequent those kinds of places," He said.

"Most of the action is dead there."

A couple of hours later they arrived back at the parking lot. He thanked her for a good time and asked if he could see her again.

They agreed to meet the next evening and she offered to have him for dinner. As he opened the door, she leaned over and kissed him on the cheek.

"Thank you for being a gentleman," She said.

"See you tomorrow evening." She gave him directions to her cottage on Tybee Island.

And as she drove away, he smiled and walked over to the rental car. *Very interesting evening, he thought.* The short drive to the hotel afforded him another look at the city. He had heard lots about Savannah, and even read some stuff on the Internet just before he had received his next assignment. Because he would be leaving via boat from the harbor, he decided that now was as good a time as any to look the area over. As he unlocked the door to his room, he thought of the next few months, and what they could possibly hold for him.

Chapter Two

• •

Rounding the bend on highway 80 into Tybee Island, the world seemed to change with every passing block. Gone was the hustle and bustle of the city life. Small shops decorated the roadsides and bungalows with many stories of days gone by dotted the horizon. Passing over the Bull River Bridge there seemed to be a quiet ambience about this area. Lazaretto Creek Road was just as easy to find as Julia said it was. As he turned onto the sand driveway at the end of the road, the cottage came into view. Pastel colors adorned the front of the house, and the wraparound porch completed the setting. As he pulled into the parking area in the front, she appeared with a glass of lemonade. He walked up onto the porch, and the delicious smell of dinner was lingering in the air.

"Ten more minutes," she said, as she stood near the rail. He couldn't help but notice the outline of her body underneath the silk shirt she wore. He had thought about her a lot last night. The sparkle in her dark brown eyes was more prevalent in the evening glow. "Special blend of lemonade?" he asked as he took the glass from her hand.

"No, just plain old lemons with a little twist of taste, a Georgia specialty." She replied. He wasn't quite as nervous as he was the night before; the late evening ride calmed the butterflies in his stomach. He sat the glass down on the rail of the porch and moved closer for a kiss. He could almost feel her heavy breathing as he caressed her. As his lips moved to cover hers, she closed her eyes and imagined a scene from her latest novel. *Slow down he thought, things are moving way too fast.* But as he attempted to pull away, she held him even closer. After what seemed like an eternity, the timer on the oven sounded and she came back to reality. As she excused herself and walked into the house to check on the food, she thought… *What was it with this guy? She had never done anything like this before. It had been a long, long time since she had been this close to a man, not to mention to invite them into her home.*

The table was set with some of the old china her mother had left her. Fresh flowers adorned the centerpiece, and the smell of the stew sitting on the old butcher-block table was very tantalizing.

"Another Georgia Specialty?" he asked.

"How did you ever guess?" She replied.

"I have never smelled such an aroma, what is it?"

"It is not polite to ask a lady what she has cooked for you. Just know that it took the better part of this afternoon, just to garner up the ingredients, and worked my fingers to the bone just preparing it." She playfully wiped the imaginary sweat from her brow as she set the food on the table. She sat down across from him and as they ate dinner, she was full of questions. Where was he from, did he have family in Savannah? How long would he be here?

By the time he was about to talk about the length of his stay, she was already pouring him another glass of lemonade. The fermented fruit in the drink was an old family recipe, and was pretty stout. They finished dinner and as she got up to clean the table, he also got up with his plate and headed towards the sink.

"I'll do that," she said.

"I am used to it," he replied, "have been doing it for over ten years now." This made her even more inquisitive. A bachelor, at least she was right, she had noticed from the start that he wasn't wearing a wedding band, and didn't even have the telltale white ring around his finger where one had been. After filling the dishwasher, she invited him to the back porch.

"The sunset is more inviting out here than in the front, and besides it is almost time for the tide to come in." Her little piece of heaven was located on the causeway and at high tide; the water almost reached the slave fence that had been there since the early days. "What brings you to Savannah?" she asked.

"I am in the United States Navy," he said.

" Next week I have to leave for several months at sea. I haven't had a vacation nor a leave in over a year, and my commanding officer thought it was a good idea for me to spend some time here before I left." I have no immediate family, so I just decided to hang around here for a while."

"Where will you be going?" she asked.

"I am not sure I can tell you that. There is some obvious tensions in some parts of the world and although I don't think you would have the means of communication with the culprits, I had rather not say."

"In other words, it is classified information, right?"

"I guess you could say that."

"By the way, what do you do besides make stranger's hearts flutter with excitement? I was almost embarrassed for you to see me staring at you last night. I wasn't being impolite, but you are one of the most beautiful women I have ever met."

"Just one of them?" she laughed."

"You know what I mean. My mother was the most beautiful woman I had ever seen, bar none. Her bright blue eyes, soft smile, and vibrant complexion made many a man sweat during her earlier years I'll just bet."

"Good Answer," she replied.

"You got out of that one quick, didn't you?"

"Practice makes perfect, I guess."

They both laughed out loud, and as she stood up to refill their glasses, a soft breeze began to blow across the porch.

"Tell me about you," he said.

"Not really much to tell, I have lived her most of my life, and after my parents passed away, I sold my condo in Savannah and moved out here to the island. Just seemed like the right thing to do. They have had this old cottage for many years, and we just used it for a weekend getaways when the town was filled with tourists. I live here alone most of the time, or at least until my brother decides to come down for a visit. Which is very seldom. He doesn't like the town, says it is about 100 years behind times and should modernize sooner or later. I like it just like it is, "Tybee Time" is a place in the world that goes by slowly and most who live here enjoy it immensely."

"What kind of profession are you in?" He asked.

"One of the oldest in the world," was her reply.

"I have a masters degree from Georgia State, but got tired of business administration and decided that I would give it up and move back here. My parents left me a little nest egg and after fixing up this old place, I decided that I would try something I had wanted to do all of my life; write novels. Lucky for me someone in New York liked them very well, and after I submitted the first one to an agent for his review, he got me an interview with a book publisher and here I am. I have written two, am presently working on the third. I have just actually started on it, but have reached a point where I have writer's block, and decided to just put it down for a while and come back to it later.

Care for a stroll?" she asked.

"Sure," he replied and they walked down the wooden steps towards the path along the causeway.

"What about you?'" she asked.

"Not really much to tell, never been married, left home at the age of 18 to join the Navy, had several tours of duty, about to embark on my final one, maybe, and hopefully when it is over, I'll probably just settle down and find a quiet little place to live. I like to tinker around with motorcycles, as a matter of fact, I have a Harley stashed at my friend's house in Jacksonville. I started to ride it up here, but decided that would be a bad idea, as I would need to have him come up here after it when I left. So I just rode the bus, got to see a lot of the beautiful country, and needed to get used to the slow mode of travel anyway. The boat I will be on is a cruiser and doesn't go very fast. "

As they started over the walkway she stopped for a moment and turned toward him. With a silly little smile on her face, she leaned forward and kissed him gently. He held her in his arms and caressed her ever so tightly. It seemed like an eternity since he had been this close to a woman. He couldn't remember the last time he had seen someone this beautiful, this close up. His affair with Victoria a couple of years ago had ended in a tragedy and he just wasn't ready to go down that road again.

He kissed her again as the wind seemed to brush through her hair. His soft touch and gentle caresses were just what the doctor ordered. She couldn't figure out what fascinated her so much about this man. From the first time she saw him, she had a warm feeling about him. She almost didn't wander out onto the balcony last night for fear of him wanting to be alone, but she was definitely glad that she had.

"We had better start back, "she said. "It gets very dark out here when nightfall comes and there are some pretty treacherous footholds along the pathway." With that they started walking back to the house. He reached for her hand and gently held it as they made their way back.

"Are you busy tomorrow?" he asked as they walked up the steps to the porch.

"What did you have in mind?" she replied.

"I have a few more days before I ship out, and would like to take in some of the sights and get the skinny on the town a little more." He said.

"Want to start out here, or in Savannah?" she asked.

"Why don't we start in Savannah and see where that leads us?" He said.

"Sounds like a plan to me." She replied. "I'll fix a picnic lunch and we can eat in the park near the old lighthouse."

"Great" he said. "I'll see you tomorrow at the statue and we can go from there."

With that he kissed her gently on the lips and walked around the house to his car. As he drove out of the driveway, she had to pinch herself. *She was puzzled. He was a great kisser, had the most gentle but sensuous touch, and hadn't made a pass at her yet. Although she was burning with desire, she didn't dare let him know that he made her tingle. What was it with this man? She had never felt like this before. Nor had she ever wanted someone so much.*

Many thoughts ran through her mind as she readied herself for bed. She took out her laptop and began making notes. She had lost complete interest in her third book and wanted to start all over with a new one. There had been many books written about her hometown, but none had the truth in them. They had all been fiction and just reeked of many paragraphs of lies and deceit.

Oh well, enough of the fantasizing, she should get to bed. As she slowly drifted off to sleep, she remembered the sparkle of his pale blue eyes as he leaned against her body when he kissed her and the rush she experienced as he held her so close. Tomorrow was another day.

As he made the turn onto highway 80 coming off Tybee Island, he couldn't help but remember the look of excitement in her eyes. *Wonder what would have happened if I had stayed a while longer? She is a beautiful woman, and is very desirable. Oh well, if it is meant to be it will, but right now is not the time to be thinking about this.*

She was there on time. He had been there for about ten minutes, enjoying a hot cup of coffee. The breeze from the river was comfortable and making her hair dance like the flight of the seagulls' overhead. Her cotton slacks and matching sweater didn't do her justice. The soft colors enhanced the dark locks and made her that much more beautiful in the early morning sun. She had parked the Chevy in the public parking lot and as she came closer she noticed his silhouette standing at the seawall. With the sun coming up in the background, he looked almost angelic in his stance. She wondered if he was really an angel, the devil in disguise; or better yet, just very good at seducing women. Making them want him from the very beginning. As he turned her way, he gave her a soft smile, and her heart melted a little more. The condition he left her in on the porch last night wasn't something she was used to. She went to bed early, but couldn't sleep. She had put away the manuscript she had started, and began to write about something else. Something that had just slipped up on her when she had least expected it.

Sometime after 3 a.m. she had fallen asleep with her laptop still on. Just before she left, she had plugged it back in to charge, as it had turned itself off sometime during her rest.

"Are you afraid of ghosts?" he asked.

"Never thought about it, she replied. "Actually I have lived close to Bonaventure Cemetery in my lifetime, but never saw any supernatural happenings."

"I understand there are some beautiful architectural buildings there." He said.

"Yes, there are some unusual designs in that place." She replied, "Sometimes in the evening as the sun is going down, you can almost see the images change. I actually used the cemetery as a place of interest in my first novel, *"The Evils of the Garden."*

"So you weren't kidding, you really write books?" He exclaimed.

"I am disappointed that you haven't heard of me. My feelings are hurt." She puckered her lip as if to act hurt. The more she puckered, the more he had to smile.

"Yes I really am an author. I have really had two published and am working on the third. I will send a copy of one with you when you leave, do you read much?" She asked.

"There are a lot of times on board ship when I am off duty that I could read, just never found anything interesting enough to capture my attention." He replied.

"I'll have to change that. When you read *Evils of the Garden*, it will keep you captivated until you fall asleep. I should know, I lost many a nights sleep writing the darned thing."

OK, let's get on with the tour." He said. As they approached the corner where the old cobblestone road meanders around and connects with Bull Street, the trolley arrived. "Bring a camera?" she asked. "Naw, Kodak apparently left out Savannah as one of their marketing locations. I have a cheap digital in the hotel room, but forgot to stick it in my pocket as I was leaving. "

"That's OK, I brought mine just in case."

"That would be good, I can download the pictures into my laptop and store them for future use."

"Planning on writing something yourself?" she chuckled.

"I don't think so,' he said. "When I was in high school I could type 57 words per minute with 6 mistakes. Now I type 6 words per minute with 57 mistakes."

She almost dropped her coffee he had bought for her. His sense of humor fascinated her.

The ride through town was very interesting to say the least. He was impressed at her knowledge of the city and its history. It seemed each one of the parks had a name and a purpose for being there. Each park had a statue, and each statue had a story. At one point he wondered if she was telling the real story or just one of hers. Once during the tour, she looked at him and simply said, "this is true stuff, not just something out of my books or imagination." She must have sensed his disbelief in some of the stories. As they passed 'the Lady and Sons" restaurant the line was out the door and almost around the block.

"I have heard that this place was really good, but I didn't think people would wait this long for a place to eat." He said.

"World Famous," was her reply.

"Her brother owns a restaurant also, but it just isn't as extravagant as this one."

"I'll just bet the food isn't as good as what you have in the basket, though."

He said with a wry smile.

"Good Answer", she said.

"Someone must have trained you just right." She laughed.

"Not really, sometimes I can come up with some things myself."

After the food discussion, things seemed to get a little more jovial. They had both let the wall down and seemed to be really comfortable with each other. Sometime in the middle of the afternoon they decided to stop in Forsyth Park and have the lunch she prepared. Homemade chicken salad sandwiches, fresh grapes, potato chips, and a slice of homemade dill pickles tantalized his taste buds.

"Fresh brewed tea?" he asked.

"Sho Nuff," she replied.

"I couldn't ruin this fine southern luncheon with some phony store bought tea. Why, I brewed it fresh this mawnin; and even squeezed the lemons myself."

"Well Ms Deveraux, I have never tasted such delightful fixins. My my, I have traveled the world over and never experienced such a fine meal." He replied with his best southern brogue. They both had a big laugh out of his mocking the southern language. As he stood to pretend to hold his smoking pipe and parade around the sitting area of the park, she couldn't help but wonder why this man didn't belong to someone. Almost tripping over a root that had been disguised by the grass, he suddenly fell onto the fine linen tablecloth she had spread for them to eat on. Blushing, he turned to face her. Her soft smile and sparkling eyes removed any embarrassment from his expression. She lay down beside him and laid her head on his shoulder. As he turned over and looked at her she softly kissed him on the cheek.

"Thank you for a wonderful day, it has been a long time since I have had so much fun." He said as he slowly stroked her hair and kissed her passionately. She returned the kiss with as much vigor and passion as he had started. Before he knew it, she had rolled over and pulled him closer. Just as he was about to kiss her again, someone called out from the other side of the picnic area.

"Julia Deveraux, is that you?"

Just as she rose up on one elbow there stood her best friend Penny Oglethorpe.

"What in the world are you doing here at this time of the day?" Penny asked.

"And who is this fine specimen of a man?"

"None of your damned business, as usual." She replied.

"Might have known the number one spinster from Jackson County Georgia would be on the prowl just about the time a girl was about to get lucky." Julia said.

Tristan didn't know whether to laugh or hide just in case the arrows were about to start flying. Penny walked over and extended her hand.

"Penny Lucille Oglethorpe, the last surviving relative to General James Oglethorpe, the visionary and military leader who established the colony of Georgia."

"Pleased to meet you mam," Tristan replied, not knowing what else to say.

"Mind if I join you, it has been a long day, and I sure could use some companionship, sure am glad I took this afternoon stroll." Penny said.

"Me too, "Julia said.

"Stroll over here near the walkway for just a minute, Penny. Tristan, I'll be back shortly."

With that Julia took Penny by the hand and led her out of hearing distance.

"What in the hell do you mean, walking up on me like that? I almost had a heart attack." Julia said.

"I thought it was you and I wasn't sure what was going on, didn't know if you were being attacked or what."

"Did I look like I was struggling?" Julia said.

"I was having a wonderful time until you barged in. Now get the heck out of here and I will call you later."

With that Penny picked up the basket she had dropped.

As she passed Tristan, she said, "Nice to meet you, hope to see you again soon."

"The pleasure was all mine, I am sure." He remarked with a laugh.

"What was that all about? Is she the local park police, or what?" He asked.

"No, just my best friend and profound old maid I guess. She has been divorced for about three years after catching her husband cheating on her with the Spanish maid, Maria. Her husband Charles came from some very old money. Penny had been employed with the county school system and met him at one of the local dances. They were only married for a short while. Most everyone around here knew that he was fooling around, except her that is; pretty much broke her heart when she found out. He gave her quite a settlement not to fight him in court. He was caught red handed and he knew it. She started an antiques store downtown, and has been doing very well ever since. We have known each other since college and have been best of friends. When my romance with my ex boyfriend went sour, she was there to bring me through it. That was some time ago and we have been president and vice president of the local man haters club since."

"Sounds like an interesting title for a novel if you ask me." He laughed.

"Tristan, I am very sorry and embarrassed. She doesn't mean any harm, she is just nosey as hell, and I get tired of her just barging in like a trooper. I cannot help it though, she really means well. And after my parents passed away, she has been there for me many times as I have for her."

"Don't apologize for me, I thought it was rather funny after I figured out she knew you. Besides, we were getting pretty close to have been in public. " He said.

"I know, I am embarrassed. I was just really enjoying your company, and I don't know what came over me." She said with a red face.

"Let's go, maybe we can find some other things to do. We have been sightseeing for the better part of the day, and I am about tired. Wish I could find a hammock. Would be nice to take a nap." They rode the trolley back to Rover Street and got into her old Chevy convertible. As she dropped him off at his car she said.

"Why don't you come out to the house?"

"Thanks for the invite, I really don't want to make a nuisance of myself, but I'd love to."

"Then follow me," she said.

"I stopped on the way in and got a bottle of wine. We can uncork it and talk some more. You know a lot about me, and now it is my turn."

"That's what I am afraid of," he said with a smile and started the car.

Following her down the highway, he wondered where in the world she had been. Most of the women he had been involved with didn't have near the sense of humor she had, and he couldn't remember when he has had such a good time. They breezed over the bridge, through town, and out to the cottage. He parked beside her and helped her with the basket and the other items she had gotten at the market on the way in. She had been to the seafood market the day before and had purchased a pound of fresh shrimp. Amanda, her next-door neighbor had graciously agreed to boil it for her and put it in her refrigerator. It was going to be her dinner surprise for herself and Tristan.

"I'll put the wine in the fridge and let it chill for a while." She said.

"Sounds like a good idea to me, now where is that hammock?" As he turned to go out the back door she gave him a quick slap on the butt and pointed him towards the corner of the yard. It had been dark when they had returned from their walk the night before and he never noticed the dock at the edge of her property. There on the walkway at the end of the dock was a double hammock.

"Where in the world did you get this?" he asked.

'It belonged to my dad. We spent a lot of time on the water and he used this a lot in his later days. After my mother died, he would come out here most every evening and reminisce about the good old days. It wasn't very long after she died, that he passed away also. I think he just died of a broken heart. You know what they say, if you have been married for a long time, you won't be separated long either. As they walked out to the end of the walkway, the evening breeze began to blow.

"I'll bet it gets cool out here in the winter, doesn't it?" He said.

"Not really, especially if you have a blanket or something warm to cuddle up with." She replied with a smile.

They sat down in the hammock and slowly let the breeze comfort them from a hard day of walking and sightseeing. As he slowly drifted off to sleep she nuzzled even closer to him than she had been in the park. They both napped for a short while and just after sunset they were awakened by the sounds of thunder in the distance.

"Storm coming?" he asked.

"Don't know, sometimes in the summer and early fall, the evening storms just happen up; especially when the humidity is high. " she said.

"Then let's go inside. Don't want to melt, do we?"

As they made their way into the kitchen she offered him another glass of tea. He declined and pulled her close to him.

"I would prefer to take up where we left off in the park", he said with a soft grin on his face. She melted into his arms as he kissed her passionately on the lips. She pressed her body closer to him than she had earlier today. She thought she could feel his heartbeat, or was it hers in the anticipation of what was in store for her? He gently picked her up and carried her into the bedroom. As he laid her on the bed, he asked where the shower was. She pointed towards the small door next to the window. As he pulled off his shirt his muscular arms diligently laid it across the back of the chair she had next to the bureau. As he was reaching for the buttons on his trousers, she came up behind him.

As he felt the smoothness of her body against his, she reached around and helped him unbutton his pants. As they dropped to the floor, she pulled him closer to her. They slowly found the bed and held each other for a long time exploring each other' s body, as the thunder in the distance was getting closer. The rain was beginning to pound on the windows, but unknown to them, as they were finally as close as they had wanted to be all day. A short time later, they lay in each other's arms, exhausted, at least for the time being.

"Care for a shower" he asked.

"Don't mind if I do, especially if you join me." She replied. As she pulled the covers back and headed toward the bathroom door, there was just enough light for him to see the silhouette of her body. Her long flowing hair against her tanned body was almost like a Divincey portrait. She turned the water on and shortly he saw a small hand motioning him to join her. The tastefully tiled shower was just big enough for the two of them and they stood in there exploring each other's bodies until the hot water ran cold. They toweled each other dry and made their way to the kitchen.

"Care for some fresh shrimp?" she asked.

"How did you know I was hungry?" he replied.

"I just figured with the extensive workout you just went through that you might need some nourishment." She answered with a soft sexy smile.

They sat at the table for a couple of hours and ate the shrimp and drank the wine. The rain finally stopped and he walked out to the back porch just as the full moon was peeking through the clouds in the cool Savannah night. The smell of the fresh summer rain still lingered in the air. As he stood there he thought of the next few months and what he had experienced here on Tybee Island. He had not had any ideas that anything like this would happen. Here he was with one of the most wonderful women he had ever met and only had four more days before he had to leave.

As he turned around to go back inside she stood in the doorway. She had lost the bathrobe she had worn earlier and walked slowly towards him. She slowly untied his towel and let it drop to the porch. She gently sat him down on the sofa and kissed him ever so gently. He could hear another round of storms in the distance, but he didn't care. Somewhere out there in the bay was the ship he was to board, but right now he was going to enjoy every minute he had with her. As their lips met, he felt the smoothness of her body against his again. The cool night winds rustled the wind chimes hanging in the corner of the porch. He ran his fingers through her hair and as they lay on the sofa, he savored every moment. Sometime during the night they retired to the bedroom for some much needed rest. As she fell asleep she nestled herself with her back against his chest, his strong but gentle arms wrapping themselves around her. He lay there for a long time pondering what to do next. His career had just escalated with his new assignment, and he knew that he could be away for quite a while. *Why had she been sent to him at this point in his life? Fate deals strange hands sometimes, and you have to play the cards as they are dealt.* He thought. The sweet smell of her hair lingered as he finally fell asleep.

The rays of the early morning sun were just peeking through the window as she walked out of the bathroom. The warm stinging of the water from the shower made her tingle even more. He had rolled over on his stomach and the sheets were barely covering his backside. She felt herself getting excited all over again and almost climbed back into the bed. A short while later she reappeared with a hot cup of coffee. As she sat the cup down on the bedside table, he rolled over and gave her a soft smile.

"Good morning sunshine," he said. "How long have you been up?"

"I don't sleep much after the sun comes up. Comes from many years of living with my dad. He always got up with the roosters and stayed up all day. My mother used to fuss at him on the weekends about getting up so early, but he would just smile and give her a cup of coffee and a kiss."

"What is on the agenda for today?" she asked.

"I'm not sure, I guess I am kind of in your care." He replied.

"Why don't we go into town and visit the Bonaventure Cemetery? " she asked.

"I need to take some pictures for research for my next book, and we can check you out of the hotel and bring your stuff back here."

He gave her a surprised look and as he sat up in the bed, she said, "I know that was a little forward, but there is no reason for you to go back and forth into the city. We enjoy each other's company, and with the short time you have left, I just want to spend some more time with you."

"Okay, then a venturing we will go." He replied. With that he pulled her down onto the bed and they playfully wrestled for a few minutes. She rolled over onto his chest and looked deeply into his eyes.

"I really don't know where this is going, Tristan, but I don't want to waste anymore time than we must. We may never see each other again, so I want to make the most of the time we have left."

He gently ran his fingers through her hair and pulled her close to him. "All right, we will go and fetch the duds, and enjoy the rest of the time I have here. I was just lying here this morning dreading having to go back to the hotel. There really is no need in me keeping the room; I am having much more fun here with you. Plus, I have been alone for quite some time, Julia, and I would be lying if I told you that I wasn't having the time of my life. You have brought a great joy to my life, thank you." She looked deep into his eyes and thought, *if you only knew what joy you have brought to me, too.*

Getting dressed and leaving the peace and solitude of her little cottage was quite a chore for him. But more than that, giving up his hotel room and spending the next two days and nights with her was an even bigger adjustment. It was OK, he thought. She was a little old fashioned, as was he. He walked around the inside of her house with a towel wrapped around him after a shower, and she did the same, only one of his shirts had been the dress for the morning for her.

He checked out of the hotel, and loaded his bag into the trunk of the old Chevy.

"I need to find a dry cleaners," he said. "My dress uniform is dirty and I'll need to make sure it is clean before I board ship. I will have to have dinner with the captain the first night out, and it is protocol for me to be dressed for the occasion."

"There is a cleaners I use quite a bit on the island, I'll make sure it gets there tomorrow. They can have it done in 4 hours if need be."

"Do you want to use the rental?" he asked.

"I have already paid for it for the week. Might as well get some use out of it."

"Not really, I feel comfortable that ole Betsey here will get us where we need to go, and if something happens to her, I have a back up."

By this time it was the middle of the afternoon and they had forgotten about nourishment. It had been quite some time since breakfast, and the fresh tomato omelets she had made didn't really go very far. The feta cheese and ham that were added were very tasty, but not much good for energy. They opted for a small seafood restaurant on the way into town. "PO PAT'S" had been a gathering place for the locals for many years. The old wooden tables and chairs outside were the perfect setting. Besides, it was getting close to the end of the summer, and the owner usually left there for warmer spots further south. Julia loved the special dishes she ate here, and wanted to make sure Tristan got some of the special shrimp dishes that were available. After a tasty meal, they were off again. As they pulled into the entrance of the cemetery, there was a plaque on the gate that gave a little of the history behind it. It seemed that Bonaventure Cemetery, which means "Good Fortune" in French, was actually the family estate of John Mulryne whom also built the third Tybee lighthouse in 1773. The family cemetery formed the nucleus of the present day Bonaventure and the rest was built around this. The live oak trees nestled on the outside edges of the dirt roadways seemed to form a tunnel through the grounds. The Spanish moss hanging from the limbs that covered the roadway cast beautiful shadows on the old monuments. As he stopped for a look at one of the small buildings, Julia coaxed him into leaning against one of the trees and took his picture. As she walked closer to him, an elderly woman passed by walking her dog. She had been watching them from a distance and thought they might be lovers.

"Can I take a picture of you two together?" she asked.

"Why certainly, that would be very nice." Julia set the camera and as she placed herself beside Tristan, he puller her close and gave her a soft kiss on the head. The lady snapped two really good pictures of them together.

"I'm not going to wind up in the pages of a love story am I?" Tristan laughed.

"Not sure," Julia replied. With me, you never know."

They walked for quite a while and decided to sit down on one of the old concrete benches that had withered with time. As they sat there talking Tristan pulled a small box out of his pocket.

"I found this in the gift shop next door to the hotel while you were getting batteries for the camera. It isn't much, but I had hoped that it would give you some pleasure when I leave."

As she opened the box, there was a locket in the shape of a seashell. As she opened the locket, she remembered her father. They spent many afternoons around the lighthouse. It had been her parent's favorite place to visit when they were alive. As a little girl, she had spent many happy evenings walking along the shore collecting shells and whatever else that had washed up on the shore. Her first book had been written about the lighthouse and how it had brought the sailors home safely in the bad storms that seemed to frequent the city. In the days of the sailboats, the lighthouse was more important than in modern times. "The Light at The End of The Bay" was her first novel, and sold over 125,000 copies. It was this story that got her a book deal for her second novel, and her friendship with her literary agent, Paul Jackson. She had started work on her third, but couldn't seem to get into it. That was the reason she was in the restaurant where she met Tristan, she had spent too much time cooped up in her cottage and needed a change of scenery, little did she know it would be this much of a change; in scenery and her life. As she looked into his eyes, she smiled and said a soft thank you. The tears in her eyes told him that this gift had touched a soft spot in her heart, but he was afraid to ask what it was. He just figured that if she wanted to tell him she could, but other than that, he wouldn't ask.

They sat there for quite awhile talking about what had happened in the last few days and what was in store for them for the next few. They decided not to talk about this any more, and just to enjoy what they had left. "The Georgia Queen leaves port at 7:00 p.m. for a dinner cruise through the city. The Savannah River is very beautiful at night. Are you up for a cruise?" she asked.

"I saw the brochure in the hotel lobby when I checked in, but didn't think I would be actually taking it. I had planned to see some of the sites around town and then take it easy for a while before I had to ship out."

"Am I too much for you?" she jokingly asked.

"No mam," he replied. "Just what the doctor ordered." He smiled and gave her a quick kiss on the cheek. They decided on the cruise and before they got into the car she asked him to secure the latch on the locket as she put it around her neck. As she started the old Chevy up, she looked over at him and simply smiled.

The Georgia Queen was docked at the end of River Street as usual. As they boarded, she handed the concierge the tickets. Tristan looked at her and said, "I didn't see you purchase those tickets."

"My treat" she replied. " This is one of the most beautiful times of the day for Savannah. The lights from the city and the sunset in the background are beyond description. I had these the other night when we met and was going to take Penny and myself but something just told me to go to the restaurant instead. I don't know how all of this happened, Tristan, but I sure am glad that it did."

The cruise was great as usual. The old Savannah buildings seemed to jump out at the river as they passed each one. "They all have a story," she said.

"I'll bet they do," he replied.

"And sometime during your career, I'll just bet you tell one or two of them."

They stood on the top deck and watched the evening sun go behind the buildings. The lights from the city gave the buildings and the scenery an iridescent glow.

Some time later the boat made it's way back to the place where they started. As they walked down the ramp the first mate gave them a complimentary Savannah Coin. On one side it had the imprint of the boat, and on the other the skyline of the city. As they got to the car he asked, "Mind if I drive?"

"Not at all," she replied. It would be nice to sit close to you. As he entered highway 80 on the way back to her cottage, she scooted over next to him and laid her head on his shoulder. The bright Savannah moon was just rising over the trees and was more beautiful than she had ever seen. There wasn't much talk on the way back to her cottage. It was almost as if they both were just savoring the time and the closeness.

As they pulled into the dirt road that led to her cottage, there was a familiar car in the driveway. There on the front steps sat Penny Oglethorpe.

"Where have you been? I have been calling you for two days."

"I don't know if that would be any of your business!" Julia replied.

Tristan excused himself, said hello to Penny as he walked into the house. As they walked around the side of the cottage for some privacy, Penny said, "What has come over you? You won't return any of my phone calls, you have been gallivanting all over town with this man that you have only known for a few days, and how long are you going to let him stay here with you? You don't know any of his background, where he is from, he might even be a serial killer and is going to rob you and leave you here to die!"

"My intentions with this man are totally none of your business. I happen to know that he is an officer in the navy, has been decorated twice for heroism, and is a very fine gentleman. He isn't married, has to leave for a tour of duty soon, and I intend to spend as much time with him as I can between now and then. He is kind, considerate, gentle, and one hell of a lover. He has touched me in places I didn't know that I had and I intend for him to touch me there again! So there, is that what you wanted to know? I saw you and Danielle Bellefonte staring at us as we walked around the cemetery today. What were you doing, following us? I know I haven't called you in a couple of days, but I have been busy with other things. He is a wonderful man, and I think I am falling in love with him."

Penny's eyes got wider and she looked as if she had seen a ghost.

"Have you lost your mind? I know I just didn't hear you say that. Why, you have been reading your own books too much. This love at first site shit just doesn't work. Remember me, I am the one who tried that, and it didn't work. Hell, you dated that idiot last summer for two months, and wound up running his ass out of town. What do you think is going to happen when this guy leaves Monday? Do you think he is going to think more of you than just a roll in the hay?"

"He isn't like that," Julia said. "I am a better judge of character than that, and if you don't mind your own business, I'll call your mother and tell her about the affair you are having with the furniture salesman from Dalton and about your little weekend trips to Jacksonville!"

"Whatever do you mean?' Penny asked.

"You know what I mean. It wasn't two weeks ago that you left with him in his shiny new convertible and there you both went. I saw the motel receipts in your purse when you came back. Remember, you left your purse wide open on your desk when I was looking at the lamps I ordered from Nashville. You have a lot of right to talk. At least Tristan isn't married!"

"Robert is in the process of getting a divorce, I saw the papers, thank you mam. He has told me all about it, many times." Penny replied.

"Really, if he is so unhappy at home why doesn't he leave?" she asked.

"I'm not going to stand out here and argue with you any more about this. Go ahead and have your little tryst with this stranger and I'll just have to have someone keep watch on you for the next few days."

"No thank you," Julia replied. "I don't need anyone to keep watch on me, especially from Tristan. Now get your ass out of here and I'll call you tomorrow."

With that Penny stormed across the lawn and threw gravel as she pulled out of the driveway.

Embarrassed, she walked up on the porch. As she opened the door, Tristan stood there. "Am I causing trouble?" he asked.

"Not at all, she is just concerned that I may be making a mistake, and is a little overprotective." She replied.

"I take it that she thought no one knew about the furniture salesman, huh?"

"Did you hear that?' She asked.

"Sure I did, I heard it all, couldn't help it. I am surprised they didn't call from the other side of the island and tell you two to tone it down a couple of hundred decibels." He said with a laugh.

"That is just great, that means that the old biddy that lives two houses down heard it and she is even nosier than Penny is. If my mother were still alive, she would already be on the phone to her giving a full report. Sometimes I think about moving, but I really like it here." Tristan took her into his arms and gave her a gentle hug.

"She is just a little unstable, I think. Both times she has given you the lecture like she is your protector or something. Thanks for taking up for me. I know I probably shouldn't be staying here. I wouldn't scar your reputation for anything. I just really like you a lot, and actually dread leaving here. But, it is something that I have to do. Lets talk for a minute."

With that they walked out the back door and sat on the porch.

"Anything you want to know about me?" He asked. "I know I haven't really told you much, but there really isn't much to tell. I have made a career out of the Navy and this is supposed to be my last tour of duty. I will probably be gone about six months, and I cannot tell you where I am going. I really shouldn't be telling you this, but I don't want you to think that I am just taking advantage of a good situation. Julia, you have made me happier than anyone ever has before. I savor every minute with you. Loving you is absolutely wonderful. Never have I had these feelings before. I cannot make any promises, but my intentions are this. I would like to come back here after my tour and continue our relationship. I know it has been a whirlwind, but it just seems right. My father and mother also passed away some time ago. They had a wonderful life together, and I would like the same thing myself. I have had two relationships in my life, but neither one of them gave me the joy that you have given me these last few days. If you will wait for me, I'll try to make sure that you won't regret it."

With tears in her eyes, she simply said, " I feel the same way. You have brought back feelings that I have forgotten. Don't pay any attention to Penny, she is still mad at her ex-husband and thinks everyone else should be as miserable as she is. She thinks Danielle Bellefonte is a good friend, but what she doesn't know is that her ex slept with Danielle also. I wouldn't want her to hear it from me, but that little troublemaker would have to go. I trust her just about as far as I could throw her little fat ass!

Is there any way we can communicate while you are gone? Are you going to be cut off from the rest of the world, or just be able to talk to your buddies, or the people on the boat, tell me Tristan, how will it be?"

"I am not sure, never worried bout it before. I never communicated with anyone other than my mother, and that was by mail. I'll be sure to try and find out how to do it, but at least we can keep in touch that way."

"If that is the case, I'll take whatever I can. Let's not think about that now, we can work on that later, right now, I want to be close to you again." She said with a smile.

"I'm going to retire to the shower and get rid of some of this fine Savannah humidity. What about you, you game for a run through the spray?" he said.

"Thought you would never ask, but let's not take too long, I have a surprise for you." As he turned on the hot water, she opened the door and stepped inside. She had brought in some bath soaps that had quite a relaxing aroma.

"Aroma therapy soap?' he asked.

"Yea," she replied, "but the therapy after the shower is what you are going to like more than this."

They finished their shower and she retired first. He stayed in and enjoyed the water a little longer. As he was toweling himself dry she returned from the living room. As he turned around there she stood. She was wearing his white uniform shirt and his hat. Except it looked a helluva lot better on her than it did on him.

"Ensign Deveraux reporting for duty sir! Do you think I could get passage on the same ship as you?" "Not in that get up sailor, I am afraid that I will have to keep you in port until I return. But let me tell you what your new orders are going to be."

She walked over to him and slowly let the shirt drop to the floor. As he pulled her closer to him, she kissed him gently. He removed the hat from her head and hung it on the bedpost, the full Savannah moon shined brightly in the sky. The rays blanketed the room with a soft shimmer. Somewhere in the bay, a naval ship was readying to sail for parts unknown. Tristan

Broward had just found a new adventure that would affect him for the rest of his life, and he wasn't going to let anything interfere with that. This wonderful woman was bringing new meaning to his life. They loved and laughed for the better part of the evening. Shortly after midnight, she fell asleep. He lay there for a short while watching her. As he slowly ran his fingers through her hair, she smiled and cuddled even closer.

❦

The rays of the morning sun glistened through the curtains. She rolled over and stretched. Reaching for him, she noticed that he had already gotten up. The tasty aroma of the coffee drifted into the room like the quiet wisps of fog over the bay. She got out of bed, meandered into the kitchen and poured herself a cup of coffee. She then walked out onto the porch. There he sat reading one of her books.

"Not bad reading," he said as she pulled out a chair across from him.

"Think the author would autograph this for me?" He said with a smile.

"Only for a small pittance," she said.

He noticed the locket she had around her neck. She hadn't taken it off since he had given it to her.

"Nice necklace."

"Someone special gave this to me, I plan on wearing it for a long time. He is about to be away for a while and I wanted him to know that I hold this very dear to my heart."

He smiled and asked if she would like some breakfast. She agreed, but said, "let's go to town for breakfast. I know this little place off Main Street that is just a short walk to the beach. The omelets are great, and the people are very friendly."

"Guess I need to put on something more respectable?" He asked.

"Nope." She replied. "Jeans and a sweater are just fine." With that he reached for his shoes and she walked to the bedroom to get dressed.

By the time they reached the "Breakfast Board Room" the morning line had grown short. Most of the tourists had eaten and gone on their way to buy trinkets, fish off the pier, or do whatever it is that they do best while on vacation. The waitress seated them near the large front windows so the morning sun wouldn't blind them. Most of the regulars were sitting at the counter, finishing up their last cup of coffee, or just milling over whatever it was they needed to do today. Just as she brought the fresh juices to their table, the waitress behind the counter answered the phone. "Billy, are you still here?" she said.

Billy Mason, the local painter of the island, was still sitting there enjoying the latest news. Seems someone had a little too much to drink at the beach last night and the police took one of the local shop owners to jail. She stretched the receiver across the cash register and told him for the umpteenth time, "Billy, you gotta get an office, or I am going to start charging you receptionist's fees. I have more to do than to answer the phone for you."

"Satellite office?" Tristan asked. "Yes, he has been on the island for about twenty five years, and most of the locals know if he doesn't answer his cell phone, he is usually sitting right there on the corner stool drinking coffee and catching up on the latest scuttlebutt of the island. Martha accuses him of staying here just long enough every day to make appointments or listen to his customers complain about not getting the work done soon enough. He simply just answers, *I'm on Tybee time, and you should be too!*

His best friend, Tony the electrician, is another of the regulars. He is here just about every morning also. They have been sitting there on that corner of the breakfast bar for longer than I can remember. Even if the place is completely full, they won't seat anyone on those two stools. They know that they will be in around 7:30 each morning, and they don't usually miss it by more than five or ten minutes." she explained.

"So what does a fellow have to do to get permanent seating around here?" he asked. "Don't know, you will have to ask Martha, the owner. She has run them out more than once but it has been quite a while since that has happened. They were mad at each other for a few weeks. Seems like they were both working on the same job once, and each one was telling the owner how great they were, and the more they talked the bigger the lies got. The owner had bought a house over on Third Street and was remodeling it for his grandmother. He thought that the boys should report to work every morning at seven and get to work promptly. After a couple of mornings of them not showing up until about 9:30 or 10:00 he finally came down here and had a really big discussion with them about their work schedules. Needless to say, he wound up firing both of them and getting someone from Savannah to come out here to finish the job."

Just as breakfast was being served, Julia looked over at the counter and Martha was pointing at their table. A young lady with a baby in one of those backpack harnesses was slowly making her way across the restaurant with a book in her hand.

"Are you Ms Deveraux?" she asked.

"Why yes I am, what can I do for you?" Julia replied.

"I bought this book in here last week and really enjoyed reading it. Would you be so kind as to autograph it for me?" she asked.

Julia's face turned a slight shade of pink as she took out her pen and signed the book.

"Thank you so much" the young mother said. "I have told several of my friends about your work, and they have enjoyed them too."

With that she turned and walked away.

"Does this happen much?" Tristan asked.

"Not really, Martha was a good friend of my mother's. They used to spend a lot of time together when my dad and Mr. Benson were in the service. After Mr. B died in combat Martha opened this little breakfast nook, and she has been here every since. Whenever I published my first book, she bought 100 copies and set them out on the counter 2 or 3 at a time. When she sold the first 100, she ordered some more and has been doing it every since. If I am in here when someone purchases a book, she always sends him or her over to me to get it autographed. It happens one or two times a month. When I published my first one, she had a special dinner for me and invited the whole island I guess. There were people lined up out the door to purchase a copy or get theirs signed. Martha sold pie and coffee until the last one was sold or signed, which was about 250 books."

As they stood up to leave, Billy and Tony stood up and started clapping their hands. This got everyone else's attention and they stood also. Julia blushed, raised her hand in appreciation and as she looked towards the kitchen, Martha gave her a thumbs up. After the festivities, they had finished their breakfast without much ado. Just about all of the patrons were from the local community and were used to the fanfare. Julia was accustomed to signing the books; she just wasn't ready for the attention in front of her new friend.

"Does this happen very much?" Tristan asked as they walked out the door.

"Two out of three times at least when I visit this place during the tourist season. Martha has been my personal publicist for the bulk of my career. I hate not to come in here, but it gets to me sometimes. Just knowing that she and my mother were good friends brings back some memories. Let's walk down to the beach, shall we?"

For the next two hours they walked on the beach. Stopping to pick up seashells, glancing at an occasional porpoise that would jump out of the water, or to sit in the old wooden swings that were placed at certain points on the walkways. They finally made their way back to the boardwalk and sat under the covered cabana at the end of it. You could see the ships going and coming across the bay. The sunlight reflecting off the tops of the waves as they slowly made their way ashore. They looked like diamonds marching towards the sandy beaches. For a long time they said nothing. Just sitting there with his arm around her and her head lying on his shoulder. After the short period of silence, she asked. "How long will it be before I hear from you?"

"Not sure, it really depends on how long the briefings take. Sometimes we are in classes for days on end finding out just where we are going and what we are supposed to be doing." He replied.

"Will you be in harm's way?" she asked.

"No my darling," he lied.

"We will just be support forces for the ground troops who will be involved in the exercise." He very well knew that he would be in the heart of the battle if it got started. For the meantime, they were just going to be back up for a peace keeping force that has been deployed to one of those far away places that no one knows about until it is too late.

He had felt some funny feelings a few days ago when he left St. Louis. He had just gotten off the cruiser that had held his attention and his residence for the last six months. He had already signed up for this mission or he wouldn't dare leave now. He had gotten closer to this woman than he had ever gotten to anyone before and he hated the thought of leaving her.

"Enough of this, let's go back. I need to make some preparations for the trip, and I should contact my friend in Jacksonville and give him some instructions. I haven't talked to him in four days, and it is highly unusual for me not to call him; especially with me about to leave." As they walked over the weathered planks on the boardwalk, the seagulls flew in circles above them. She reached out and took his hand and held it until they made it to the parking lot. As they walked down the street towards the restaurant, she could see the old Chevy sitting on the side of the road. They stopped by the cleaners where she had left his uniform, and made a refreshment stop at the corner market also. When they pulled into her driveway, she felt a little uneasy. She had spent the last few days with one of the most wonderful men in the world. Now he will be leaving for how long she did not know. Would he be back, what were his intentions? Was this just a little fling for him before he shipped out? Many questions ran through her mind. As they walked up the stairs he opened the front door for her. He leaned forward and gave her a soft kiss on the cheek. He took the groceries from her hands and as she opened the door he said, "I need to tell you something." Her heart sank; *here it comes, she thought;* most bad news comes after a statement such as that. She could almost feel the color changing in her face. Tristan also noticed the concerned look she was giving him. He took her hand and led her out onto the back porch.

"I know we haven't known each other very long, but I am very fond of you. You have made me the happiest man in the world for the last week. I never intended to come down here and fall in love, but I think that is just what has happened. I would very much like for you to wait for me until I finish this mission. I don't know if you are attached to someone else; although I really doubt that you are in any type of committed relationship, or you wouldn't have gotten so close to me for the last few days. I guess what I am saying is that I really want to continue this whatever we have as soon as I get back. I really don't know how long I will be gone; it could be three months and maybe longer, maybe shorter, depending on what comes up. I probably won't be able to call you much, however we can communicate via e-mails, letters, or maybe even an occasional call if we get out of a secured area. I just want you to try to understand my situation. I promise I will come back to you as soon as I can. I just don't know when that will be. I know you have lots of stuff on your mind right now, but know this, I really want to pursue this relationship of ours."

Tears of joy filled her eyes. "I want the same thing, Tristan. I am not involved with anyone else as I have told you, and haven't been for a long, long time. I sense that we have something special here, and I too want to continue it. I will wait for you as long as it takes."

She stood up and melted into his arms. He picked her up and carried her through the house to the bedroom. He was happy beyond all belief. After some time, they drifted off to sleep in each other's arms; they both were more satisfied than they had ever been in their lives.

A couple of times during the night they got up for refreshments, only to retire back to the bedroom. If he was going to be gone for a while, she was going to take advantage of whatever time she could have at the moment. The alarm sounded at precisely 6 a.m. He had already told her that he had to be at the port no later than nine. He was already up, dressed in his uniform, and packing his bag. She had envisioned him in uniform, but he was more handsome than her dreams.

"Got to get a move on," he said. "I cannot be late. Although my thoughts have run rampant of getting there just as the smaller craft is leaving to take us out to the ship, hoping I could be late and they would forget me, but I don't think that will happen. They would just send the boat back for me and I would start out in trouble with the captain."

"How many will be leaving from here?" she asked.

"Not sure," he replied. " I haven't seen any evidence of a lot of sailors in town, but that doesn't mean anything, they could be coming from anywhere. Another thing, I am also a member of a SEAL team. Do you know who they are?"

Her heart stopped. She had been the daughter of a naval commander and she knew who the Seals were, she just never thought she would be involved with one.

"Is this one of a long list of assignments you will be given for the rest of your life?" she asked.

"No, this is the last one if I want it to be, and believe me, I do want it to be the last one. I have been around the world four times, and I am ready to settle down, with you if you will wait for me. I really don't think this will be a dangerous mission, but I had to tell you all about me, I don't want you to think I lied about anything. I want to be completely honest with you. I have never wanted anything any more in my life."

Two hours later they were standing at the pier. "I will contact you as soon as I can." He said.

"I know, darling, I trust that you will." She said.

"Now you need to leave so I can. The smaller boat will take me out to the ship."

"What is the name of the ship?" she asked.

"Not for you to know, you already know more than you should. I should have never told you this much. I don't want you to worry, and telling you the name of the ship won't help matters either. Besides, I may transfer to another ship anyway. Just trust me, everything will be all right."

She gave him a long kiss and hugged him ever so tightly. He kissed her passionately and grasped the seashell locket between his thumb and forefingers. "Whenever you think of me, just rub this locket; it is filled with love."

As he turned away to walk towards the ship she said," I love you."

He turned around and gave her that wonderful smile, the same one he gave her standing on the balcony of the restaurant that first night. He boarded the smaller boat and they headed out to the larger ship in the bay. As he disappeared into the waves, she held the locket he had given her. Tears streamed down her face. Fear and wonder filled her heart. She had written these feelings into one of her books, but she never dreamed that she would be feeling them herself. As she walked towards the old Chevy, there was an envelope on the front driver's seat. When she opened it, she realized it was from Tristan. He had apparently penned the note inside earlier that morning, as he was getting ready to leave.

The inside of the card simply read:

> These last few days have brought much joy to my heart. I have experienced feelings only you could have given me. Please take care of yourself and we will be together again,
>
> I promise.
>
> Tristan

The drive back to Tybee Time was lonely, but she had a renewed faith in her life; and a new direction. These last few days had given her a renewed spirit in writing. Her writer's block was gone; she had many thoughts and ideas in her head and was ready to transform them into words. Just as she turned into the dirt road to her cottage, she got a phone call from Penny.

"Well, are you going to have some time for your friends this week, or has Mr. wonderful got you booked this week too?"

"No smart ass," Julia replied. "Get your butt over here, we've got a lot to talk about."

Penny couldn't wait to hear the goodies. As she rounded the curve on River Street headed to Tybee Island, she remembered that she owed Julia a bottle of wine. She stopped at the downtown liquors and purchased a bottle of Davenport Red, one of Julia's favorite tastes. She knew it would take most of the night to get the skinny on everything that had happened, so she cancelled her pedicure. She wouldn't miss this for anything in the world. Julia had changed into a linen shirt and a pair of canvas shorts. The cool evening breeze was blowing and the tide would be coming in soon. They broke open the bottle and sat down in the swing on the dock. "I don't care where you begin, just don't leave anything for the imagination, girl," Penny said.

"I don't know where to start, but I can tell you one thing; I am in love with him."

Chapter Three

Tristan's quarters on the cruiser were small and cramped as usual; but he knew he wouldn't be there long any way. His orders when he boarded the ship were to rendezvous with his other Seal Team members two days out to sea. He would then be transferred via helicopter to an aircraft carrier off the coast of some god-forsaken country that still thinks they own the world. The worldwide terrorist organizations had been meeting on this tiny little island for the better part of three weeks. The intelligence had been transmitted to Tristan via a satellite link he kept in his duffle bag. Lucky for him that Julia was a heavy sleeper or he wouldn't have gotten the last messages. He had taken a big chance staying with her these last few days but it was worth the risk. As he unpacked his bag getting ready for the transfer, he found one of her books stashed inside. The inscription on the inside front cover read:

Tristan,

Keep this for the times when you are out to sea and are thinking of me. You hold a special place in my heart and I will keep you there until we meet again.

Love,

Julia

Dammit, it was going to be hard enough after this week, but she had to write one of those gushy notes in the book. What a girl! It hadn't been one day and he was already missing her. The bright Georgia moon was coming up over the horizon and he thought of her in his uniform shirt and hat. Inside the book, she had taped a small photograph of herself in his shirt and hat. The inscription simply read:

Ensign Deveraux reporting for duty. Will be awaiting your safe return.

He read for a while, and finally put the book down. He had an early meeting with the captain the next morning, and he dare not be late. As he closed his eyes he could see the silhouette of her beautiful body standing in the doorway of her bedroom; the place they spent most of the last day he was there.

Several miles away she sat in front of her laptop banging away. Her heart was filled with joy and her mind racing with ideas. She had started research on her latest idea for a book. The one she had been working on had been put to the wayside to be finished later. The idea was good at the time, but a better one had replaced it. The soft rays of the moon beamed in as she put the special lemonade back into the fridge. She had just finished her snack and was nestling down to her work. It would be a while before she would get a good night's rest again. She wouldn't until she had finished the book. That was the only thing she had problems getting used to. It is hard to rest when you are in the writing mood. It just seems like you are obsessed with finishing it. She had spent almost five hours with Penny Oglethorpe quizzing her about any information she could get on her ex-husband's ancestors. She had decided to write a love story that would happen in the early days of the confederate war. Savannah had been the setting for the beginning of her love story with Tristan, so she had decided that her newest work would be set during that time in history. She would have to come up with a title later, right now she had too many other ideas to work on. Penny had been gone for just a short while. Steaming and furious, she thought she was going to get the four one one on everything that had happened between Tristan and Julia for the last week. Boy was she surprised. Every time she would ask Julia an intimate question, Julia would fire one back about her husband's family tree during the civil war, or whom she thought would make a good character for her book. Penny was great with imaginary names. She had learned from the best. Her ex husband was deeply into role-playing and Penny had been everything from a cocktail waitress to the local schoolteacher. The names were changed to protect the innocent. She would go to the library in Savannah tomorrow and gather some information on the civil war and the south. She had considered doing this once before when she had some extra time, but couldn't come up with a story line. That had all changed in the last few days. She had one hell of a story to tell now. A southern debutante's affair with a confederate spy in the civil war. She couldn't wait. And what better place for it to happen?

Chapter Four

....

As he entered the captain's quarters, he noticed that they weren't alone. There was someone there that he had never seen. He had been on Captain Morgan's ship once before in his career and it had been a pleasurable stay. The Somerset; as it was called; had picked up his team from another forgotten place in the world and had transported them back to civilization. It had taken them the better part of a week to complete the journey, and Tristan had loved every minute of it. It wasn't his idea of a cruise, but it was the next best thing. As he stood at attention, the captain and the visitor both saluted him.

"Be seated" the stranger said. "Thank you, I believe I will." Tristan replied.

"Sergeant Broward, you and your team have been chosen to participate in a very complicated mission. One of our operatives has been working within one of the largest terrorist organizations in the world. They are meeting on San Cabbala Island as we speak. Our operative has some very sensitive information that we need to process for what seems to be another attack on

American soil. We need you and your team to extract him as soon as possible."

"Yes Sir, I understand the urgency," Tristan replied, " but if you have all of them together on one island, why don't you just take them all out, and be done with it? It seems like you guys have been waiting for this opportunity for a long time; why not take advantage of it while you can? The last briefing I was in on the status of these things was that there was to be a summit meeting with all of them and that they were planning something really big."

"You have most of it right, they are planning something, but we just don't know what exactly it is. The only way we can find out is to get this guy back home, and get the information from him. He also supposedly has some information on the whereabouts of a certain terrorist leader that we have been searching for a long time. Are you game Sergeant?"

"I certainly am, sir, but I don't believe we have ever met."

"We don't need to meet, and as a matter of fact, this meeting never happened. In this file is all of the information you will need. You will meet with the other members of your team tomorrow and go over the intelligence. After that you have thirty six hours to put a plan together, because at about that time you guys will be riding a slow raft to the east side of the island."

"Thank you, sir" Tristan said as he stood. "I will have the information analyzed by then and have a plan in action. Thank you for the opportunity to serve my country again."

With that he saluted the captain and walked out the door. After he had left, Captain Morgan and the "General" we are alone in the cabin.

"Do you think he can get the job done," the general asked.

Captain Morgan replied. "From what I know personally and have heard about this young man, you can pretty well count on it, sir."

Tristan retired to the operations room of the Somerset, and started looking over maps, gps coordinates, and any other information he could find on the island. After the extraction, they were to be picked up by a nuclear submarine a few miles off the coast and transported back to the Somerset for debriefing. As he was making notes, captain Morgan met him in the operations room. "Congratulations, lieutenant." The captain said.

"I think you may have made a mistake sir, I haven't been promoted in several years." "That is until today," the captain said. "Here are your lieutenant's bars, wear them proudly. There will be a formal presentation after the mission. Just be sure that you are there to receive it." With that the captain left Tristan alone with the surprise and the information the general had given him.

What a week he thought. Meeting Julia, getting this mission, and a promotion; what a lucky guy I am! About that time there was a knock on the door. As he opened it there stood his right hand man, Sergeant James Wilson. "Big Jim" as he was called, stood over six feet six inches tall and weighed in at about 255 pounds. There wasn't much fat on him either; it was almost all muscle. They both had been on too many missions to count in the last five years, and they were getting few and far between. Jim had bought some land in alligator alley and was planning on starting a farm but had been too busy to get it started.

"The rest of the crew will be here tomorrow, sir. Congratulations on the promotion." he said.

"How the hell did you know about the promotion, I just got the damned bars not more than thirty minutes ago." Tristan said with a puzzled look on his face.

"Guess good news travels fast, huh?" he replied.

"Did everyone make the cut?"

"All of us are together again, with the exception of Jared, he wrecked his bike a couple of weeks ago and he will be down for the count for at least two months. He was riding through some little Tennessee community and just lost it. He said he looked behind him and the next thing he knew, he was rolling on the asphalt. Probably checking to see if some jealous husband was chasing him. Bad timing for a wreck, there aren't too many electronic wizards like him left in this business. We will miss him I am sure." Big Jim said.

"Oh well, maybe he just needs and extended vacation. We'll catch him on the next one. We need to get to work on this information and see just how we need to break up this little party. The operative will be on the south side of the island at the pick up time, and we need to make sure that we get there and get him out. Here are the maps and the surveillance photos, let's get to work on this so we can get outta here tomorrow night."

For the next few hours they went over the maps, grids, and photos of the island. Sometime after midnight after Jim left for some much needed rest.

Tristan walked outside for a long while. Staring at the reflection of the moon on the smooth water, he thought of Julia. She would be lying halfway uncovered with her long black hair flowing across the pillow. To think, just a couple of days ago she was lying on his arm, nestled close. Gosh, he missed her. Never had he had so much fun in such a short period of time; not to mention the fact that no one had ever made him feel this way before, either. The moonlight glistening off the waves, reminded him of the sparkle in her eyes. Even through the tears in her eyes as they parted at the port they still had the sparkle. His mind wandered back to the hammock on the dock on the outskirts of Tybee Island, and the sweet smell of her perfume in the soft evening breeze.

A short while later, he retired to his quarters; knowing he couldn't stay awake all night, he had a very important mission to accomplish. He and big Jim would leave the rest of the crew after they reach landfall and retrieve the agent.

The next day was spent preparing the necessary supplies for the mission. They were to take off shortly after sundown and would be dropped off from a low flying helicopter to avoid radar interference. "Remind you of anything?" big Jim asked as he handed Tristan a cup of coffee.

"What are you talking about?" Tristan replied.

"You know what I mean, you were looking out at the helicopter and the guys loading the gear on it. It reminds me of the time we were sent to Colombia to get the girl."

"Yes, you are right, the scenery is almost the same, isn't it?

Tristan took a long sip of the coffee and walked back into his quarters. He took out the book Julia had written the inscription in. He read the short note again, thinking of what she might be doing and how much longer it would be before he could see her again. As he stuffed it back into the duffle bag, the captain called over the intercom, "Time to mount up." Tristan took the Beretta that his dad had given him for his 30th birthday and shoved it into the shoulder holster. As he walked out onto the deck he smiled at his thoughts of her.

The library was unusually busy for this time of the morning. There were lots of younger people in here than she had noticed before. Also it had been quite some time since she had been here also. She had to wait a few minutes to use one of the computers so she browsed around in the Civil War section looking for anything that might interest her. A short time later she was able to sit down and research the database of information about what she was looking for. Two hours and a few dollars later, she had about 37 pages of information she had downloaded from the computer's database. Information on battles, confederate soldier information, and just general "stuff" about the war that she would need for her novel that lay on the seat beside her. As she drove the old Chevy towards Forsythe Park she wondered where Tristan was and what he was doing at this point in time. As her thoughts roamed across the ocean, she touched the locket she wore around her neck. She had taken one of the pictures that another visitor had graciously taken of them together in Bonaventure Cemetery and had it resized so it would fit in the locket. Occasionally she would open it up just to get another look at him. *Life had many twists and turns, she thought. But it had taken a u-turn for her. She had gone from being alone and not needing anyone, to being in love. How could it happen in such a short time? She wasn't sure, but one thing she was sure of; she was very glad that it did.*

Penny Oglethorpe spread the tablecloth over the picnic table near the statue and set the basket on the table. As she took the cheese and wine out, Julia came strolling up the walkway with a big smile and a new pep in her step. Penny turned around and as Julia reached the table she said with a laugh, "I hate you, you bitch. You are purposely holding back on me. You know I am also jealous of you. Here I have been chasing trousers for the last three months and only can connect with losers. You, on the other hand, go to a restaurant and find one of the most wonderful men in the world, or so you say. I never even got a chance to talk to him to check him out for you."

"I know, but I am glad that you didn't; he is a great guy, not to mention a wonderful lover. " Julia teased.

For the next three hours, they sat and talked about Tristan. Julia finally gave up and told Penny most of the story. She even admitted that she was a little afraid that he wouldn't come back.

"Things like this happen only in story books," she said. "But I am going to wait and see. You never know, he may show up tomorrow. All I know is this; I have never felt this way about anyone else. He has given me memories that I will never forget, and I surely will never forget him."

They packed up the basket and walked towards the parking lot. As they approached Penny's Cadillac she said. "By the way, when are you going to get a decent car? I know you are making enough money on the royalties from your book, and also you still have most of the money your parents left you, don't you? You need to get rid of that old junk pile."

"Mind your own business,' she replied. "I am very fond of this old piece of junk as you call it. Besides, it is paid for and gets me where I need to go. It also fits in to the environment that I live in. I even thought of getting a license plate that says Tybee Time, but it has too many letters in it. Just leave me alone, I'll get a new one when I want to, and mind your own business." Little did Penny know that she had already purchased herself another vehicle. She knew the old Chevy wouldn't last much longer, and she really needed to have dependable transportation. She had parked it in the basement of her parents old home out on the island and kept it covered. The home was another part of her life she needed to deal with. The house was in good condition and although no one lived in it, she should really think about moving back into it on a permanent basis. Maybe it would be some place she and Tristan could spend some time together. Bt there was plenty of time for that later she thought.

"Let's take a carriage ride. So we can talk some more" Penny suggested.

"You mean so you can ask me some more questions about Tristan, don't you?" Julia replied.

"Well, if you must put it that way, you are right. I want to know what it is about him that has you so gooey and wide eyed. I haven't seen you this happy in years. I hate to admit it, but I am almost jealous. If anyone should be happy, it should be you; with all that you have gone through in the last few years. Just be careful and don't get yourself hurt like you did the last time." she warned.

"That was another lifetime ago, that I had almost forgotten about it. So let's not go there again."

For the next two hours, they had discussions about most everything. The anticipation of families, children, marriages, and just about every other lifelong opportunity that they could think of came up. Finally Penny admitted that she was unhappy with life as it was, and was seriously on the hunt for a husband. "I guess if I am going to find one, I am going to have to go elsewhere." She said. "Everyone here knows about my past, and I guess I will never live it down. After spending the day with you and observing the joy you have received, I am happy for you. I really feel that you may have found something here. I just hope that someday I should be so lucky."

The rays of the sun were passing through the Spanish moss on the trees. As they passed through what seemed like the natural tunnels in the streets they agreed that they should get back to reality and do this again, soon. The carriage returned them to the parking lot where they had met and left them to their memories. Penny's of how happy Julia seemed to be, and Julia's memories of the carriage ride she had taken with Tristan just a few evenings before. *My how things have changed she thought;* little did she know that her life was about to be changed even more. She gathered the information from the old

Chevy that she had gotten at the library and walked into the little cottage on the causeway. She poured herself a glass of the special lemonade that she savored so dearly. One of the many things her mother had taught her during her lifetime was how to make this special taste for the lemonade, funny how she thought of her at this time. As she walked out onto the boardwalk, the soft evening breeze rustled her hair. She sat on the hammock that she and Tristan had lay in for so long. As the sun was going down, she closed her eyes and remembered his soft touch and wonderful caresses. She walked back to the house, turned on her computer, and traveled back to the days of war and love; *the days that made the setting for the town of Savannah. The war was raging, and so were the passions of the two main characters in her book; the lady and the confederate soldier. Just before the attack on Fort Savannah, they were enjoying an intimate meal overlooking the water. She had spent the better part of two hours getting ready for this. Here she sat with the most handsome soldier in the confederate army; his long hair loosely clinging to the collar of his coat. As he sat down he elegantly removed the sword and it's scabbard and sat it beside the table near the rail.*

"No need for this, I am sure." He said.

"No," she replied. "That is the last thing you will need before this night is over."

The waiter poured them each a glass of wine, and just as he reached for her hand, there was a loud explosion. Julia had no more than finished typing this sentence, than she had a very disturbing feeling come over her. Suddenly she felt as if something was wrong. She got up from her desk and walked over to the window. There was an evening storm brewing and she could see the lightning in the distance. As she looked into the sky she said a silent prayer;" Please let him be ok dear God,

I know that he was the answer to my prayers for the longest time, don't give him to me and then take him away so quickly."

⁂

The loud whisper of the rotors pierced the soft evening air. As they boarded the helicopter they checked their weapons and ammunition for the last time before contact with the enemy. Tristan and Big Jim were going over the last minute plans making sure everyone knew what their job would be and where they were to do it. They would be dropped just off shore and swim to the island. Tristan and Jim would find the agent, bring him back to the raft, and they would then find the submarine to take them all back home. It sounded like a simple extraction. A couple of hours later, about twenty-five feet above the water, the helicopter hovered. As usual Tristan would go first; he turned and looked at the others giving them the same look of reassurance as he had done on their last ten missions, all of which had been successful. He jumped into the dark waters below and just as he hit the surface, a deafening sound and a blinding flash of light stunned him. The last thing he remembered seeing was the helicopter exploding and falling toward him. Just as Tristan hit the water big Jim saw it. The surface to air missile had been fired from the island, giving them no time to react. As he looked into the frightened faces of the rest of the seal team, he knew that would be the last thing he would ever see again. Captain Morgan chewed the end of his cigar. He had quit smoking five years ago, but just couldn't quite give up the habit of having one around. His love for cigars was only second to his love for the service. As he turned to walk away from the radar screen, the image of the helicopter faded away.

"Sir, I think we have a problem." The radar technician said.

"What is going on?" the captain replied.

"We have just lost contact with Tiger 2. She had stopped and all of a sudden there is no contact with her, visually on the screen, or over the secure radio channel."

"Where in the hell is the sub?" the captain asked.

"About twenty miles from the site, sir."

"Tell them to get their ass over there and see if there are any survivors, and do it now!"

Chapter Five

As Jared Olson steered his pickup in to the Mustin Road entrance to Jacksonville Naval Hospital he still couldn't believe what had happened two days before. Still sore and stoved up from the motorcycle accident, he walked carefully not to twist his knee any more than he could help. Learning the correct way to walk on crutches was one of the hardest lessons he had ever needed to learn. The doctor had told him to stay off of it for six weeks, but after hearing about the incident with his team, he couldn't just sit back. Was it a twist of fate that he had wrecked his motorcycle, was someone telling him that he needed to quit, or was it just everyone's time but his to cash in the chips? By the time he made it to the elevator in the lobby he was already sweating. The latest report on Tristan was that he had a concussion from the blast, and that he had not regained consciousness. He had been unconscious since the explosion. The submarine had picked him up shortly after the explosion, and luckily for him the flotation device on his life preserver pack was inflated and kept his face out of the water. He had a small cut on his forehead from the shrapnel, but everything else had been checked out and seemed to be in good shape. Jared had gotten a call from the "General" and was told that he needed to get to the hospital in Jacksonville Florida as soon as possible. He sat in a chair next to the bed and leaned his crutches against the wall. There lay his friend and commanding officer bandaged with a breathing tube coming out of his mouth. A few minutes later, the nurse came in and asked whom he was. Jared explained that Tristan and he were good friends.

"Is there anyone we need to call?" she asked.

"Not that I know of," Jared replied. "Did he have any personal belongings with him when he was brought in?"

"The only thing we have is his duffle bag which was brought in by a Captain Morgan. He said that was all that Lt. Broward had with him when he boarded the ship. I don't know any of the particulars other than that." She explained.

As she turned to go out of the room, Colonel Jackson Barker entered. Jared recognized him from the portrait in the lobby, as he reached for his crutches to stand and salute the commanding officer of the hospital Colonel Barker told him to stand at ease.

"Do you know what happened?" the colonel asked.

"No, I just got a call from someone telling me that Tristan was here and that I probably needed to come down. We don't really have a location that we are permanently assigned to, so that is about all I feel comfortable telling you."

The colonel walked to the door and closed and locked it. As he walked back toward the bed he opened the closet and took out Tristan's duffel bag. He handed it to Jared and asked, "Do you know what happened?"

"The information that was given to me was that they were in the middle of the assignment when something went wrong and there was an explosion. That is all that I know. The news is reporting that the helicopter was on a routine mission when it collided with something killing all of the passengers on board. That is about it. I am guessing that a surface to air missile got them before they could get out of the chopper. Was there any retaliation?"

"Only that the agent that they were on the way to pick up had been tortured to death and hung from a tree. Most of the big boys had left just shortly before the helicopter got to the location and the only ones that were left were just guards on the island. By the time the F-22 Raptors got there, there wasn't much good in trashing the whole island, they just destroyed the buildings and the airfield. If these bastards use this place again, it will cost them a hell of a lot of money to make it usable." The colonel said.

"By the way, got any idea who Julia Deveraux is?"

"Never heard of her, why do you ask?" Jared said.

The colonel handed Jared a book that had been found in Tristan's personal belongings.

"I know Lt. Broward had no living relatives, but I think you might want to try to find this lady. From the information that is written in this book, and the letter he had written to her, seems like they were having some sort of relationship. There are some pictures of her and an address. It may not be a bad idea to try to get in touch with her."

"Lt Broward?" Jared asked.

"That's right," the colonel replied.

"He got his bars just before he left for this mission. From what I have learned about this guy, they were a long time coming. How many missions have you been on with him?"

"This would have been the tenth." Jared replied.

"Our team had been together for the better part of five years. The reason I wasn't on that chopper with the rest of them was because I wrecked my motorcycle and was under a doctor's care. Was he the only survivor?"

"That's the way it looks son, they haven't found all of the parts to the chopper yet. There is no way anyone could have survived an explosion like that. The only thing that saved him was that he had just jumped and was under the surface when the missile hit. The concussion of the blast and the explosion knocked him out. The submarine found him floating on top of the water and he was airlifted here. He hasn't been awake since. I was about to try to contact the lady when you arrived. It may be a good idea for you to find her and bring her here. I have a feeling she is going to want to come here anyway. There is nothing you can do here. He is in apparent good physical health, just in a coma. Surgeons say he should come out of it in a few days, but they don't know exactly when. It is a two-hour drive from here to Savannah where this lady apparently lives. If you get a move on, you can be there before dark. There is an envelope with directions to her house. Go get her, or at least tell her what happened."

"Yes sir," he replied.

Julia and Penny had spent the better part of the day shopping in Savannah. She hadn't heard from Tristan in almost two weeks and needed some reassurance. Shopping was a good way to get your mind off of anything bad, as Penny would say. Besides she had spent the last few days and nights working on her newest book and still didn't have a title for it. She had been worried about not hearing from Tristan, but he had told her before he left that he may not be able to talk to her for a while. She had received one e-mail message from him, but when she tried to send one back it came back undeliverable.

As they turned on the dirt road leading to Julia's house they noticed the bright red truck parked in her driveway. There was a man sitting on her front steps, clutching a book.

"I'll just bet he wants an autograph." Penny said.

"I have had some requests to sign my books in some pretty unusual places, but never had anyone come to my house to do it. Wait a minute, that can't be right either, this place is still in my parent's names, there is no way he could know unless he is a local, and I have never seen him or that truck around here." Julia replied.

They parked beside the truck and as they got out of the old Chevy, he stood up.

"Can I help you with something, or are you just lost?" Julia asked.

"No mam, my name is Jared Olson and I am a friend of Tristan's." he said as he handed her the book. She opened it and realized it was the one she gave him the day he left. All of a sudden she felt weak and her knees almost buckled. Something was terribly wrong.

"Where is he, is he all right, what has happened?" she asked with a troubled tone in her voice.

"Come over here and sit down." He replied. Julia sat down on the porch beside him with tears in her eyes. Penny stood by the car not wanting to believe any of this.

"Tristan is in the naval Hospital in Jacksonville Florida. I left there this afternoon to come here and tell you. He was involved in an accident and is in a coma. I will take you there. My name is Jared Olson and I am in the same unit as he is. I brought the book because you apparently signed it for him. Also, I have this picture of you and him. I figured you would be more likely to believe me if I had these with me. According to the doctor's report he had a concussion from the blast but otherwise he is in good health no broken bones or contusions. He does have a small cut on his head, but nothing serious.

"Can I see some identification?" she asked.

"Sure," he said. He produced his military I.D. and also his driver's license.

"Thank you, now tell me what the hell is going on. What kind of blast are you talking about and how did you find me? Nothing at this location is listed in my name, and the car is also listed to my parents. Now do you want to tell me what this is all about?" she said.

"Do you want to see him, or do I just leave and go back to where I came from? I can get you into the hospital to see him, but you have to go with me. They just won't let anyone go in there without a security clearance, not on that floor anyway. The hospital commander sent me here, I can go back and tell him that you didn't want to come, is that what you want me to do? I can tell you on the way, or we can stand here and take the time to hash all of this out. If it was me, I would be more inclined to go."

"I am sorry," she said. "It's just that this is something that is hard to swallow. I haven't heard from him in almost two weeks and we had just gotten acquainted when he left."

"I know, he is my best friend and commanding officer. We have been together for a long time, it is hard to see him in this condition."

"Let me throw some clothes together and I will be ready shortly." Julia said.

"Have you lost your mind?" Penny asked. "Are you just going to take off with this guy on a whim with a story like that? How do you know he is telling the truth? He could be some kind of stalker or even worse. You are just going to take off with him on a two hour drive that will end up God knows where?"

"His credentials are real, or at least they look real." She said.

"How do you know, have you ever seen real government documents?"

About that time, Jared walked over to Penny and handed her his cell phone. "The number to the hospital is on the screen. The commanding officer will answer this line and you can ask him. But let me ask you something, how do you think I got these pictures or this book that she autographed for him and also wrote him an intimate note inside? I know this sounds crazy, but I am just trying to do what was suggested to me by the commanding officer of the hospital. If you would like, you can follow me with her in the car and that way everybody will be safe, ok?"

About that time Julia ran outside with her suitcase in her hand. "Let's go," she cried. "Time is wasting. I don't want anything else to happen to him and me not be there. The identification is obviously real, or he wouldn't be able to know as much about me as he does. If he fabricated all of this, then let it be; but this story is to far fetched not to be real. Penny, get some clothes and head toward the hospital. I am going to ride with Jared so I can get the whole story behind all of this."

They waited a short while for Penney to pack some clothes and took off. As they crossed over the bridge onto the main highway she looked at him. They hadn't spoken much in the last fifteen or twenty minutes.

"Ok, give it up," she said. "I want the whole story from the beginning."

"How much do you know about him," he asked. "Or better still, how long have you known him?"

"We met in a restaurant a couple of weeks ago. We hit it off really good and spent the rest of the whole week together. He stayed with me for the last three days 24-7. I don't know what came over me, as I never let that happen before. He was very kind and gentle, very well mannered, and knew how to make a woman feel good. I fell in love with him; I absolutely fell about as far as you can fall in love with him. When he left that morning he promised that he would call me or contact me as soon as he could. He never called, although I did get one e-mail message from him. When I tried to reply, it simply said that he was unreachable. What kind of e mail service does the damned government have, anyway?" She asked.

"A very secure one," he answered. "That doesn't surprise me. I hardly ever use the service, for that very reason. Most of the messages are edited for content, especially if it gives any kind of information as to where you are or what you are doing. I have sent messages to my dad that simply said that I was ok, and would be home when I could. What is the scoop on your friend? Can she be trusted? We are going to an area that is secure and they will probably give her some pretty intense questioning. You have already been checked out pretty good and have clearance."

"So who are you guys anyway, the CIA? Tristan didn't say much about what he was going to do, he just simply told me that he was a gunnery sergeant and would be on the ship for no telling how long. That he would contact me as soon as possible. So jump in her anytime and tell me what is going on! I have enjoyed just about as much of this suspense as I can stand; and I know this security stuff is important, my father was in the Navy himself."

"They know, that is why you got the security clearance as fast as you did. The hospital commander was in the service with your father, he knew him personally. I think that is another reason that he sent me for you. Tristan was the team leader for the number two Seal Team in the world. We had all been together for about five years and have completed missions all over the world. The only reason I wasn't on this assignment with them was because I wrecked my motorcycle and was under a doctor's care for my knee injury. When Tristan boarded the ship he had a meeting with the captain and a very high-ranking official of the United States government. He is affectionately known as the "General". He has been involved in most of the really important missions concerning national security. Anyway, after the meeting with those guys, Tristan was promoted to Lieutenant. He was given the choice of completing this mission or just simply going to Washington for a couple of months. He opted to complete the mission and have the option to choose his assignment of duty after that. He has a diary that he has kept for the last ten years. It has some pretty secure information in it. It was confiscated when his personal items were taken from the Somerset. I don't know if it will be destroyed or what will happen to it, but more than likely it won't surface anywhere. They don't like stuff like that to get out." He explained.

"So tell me about the accident, or whatever it was."

"This is very confidential, you cannot tell anyone, even Penny. If you repeat any of this I could get court-martialed. Tristan and the rest of the members of our team were on a recovery mission. They were to fly to this small island and retrieve an operative that had been under cover in a terrorist organization for two years. As they approached the drop point, Tristan went first as usual. As he hit the water, a missile fired from somewhere around the island hit the helicopter and killed everyone on board. The helicopter burst into flames and was blown into many small pieces. The force of the blast was tremendous and he would have been injured more seriously had he not been under water. The operative was found a few hours later inside one of the houses on the island. He had been dead for quite a while. More than likely he was dead before they even left to rescue him. Tristan has a small cut on his head with a few stitches, but that is apparently all. Other than being in a coma. The doctors say his brain is swelled and that is the reason for his problem. They anticipate him waking up, they just don't know when. They were considering surgery to relieve the pressure when I left. The fact that he had no living relatives made the decision difficult. They don't usually do that under those circumstances unless it is a matter of life or death. All of his vital signs were good when I left. The CO told me that if anything changed he would call, and I haven't heard from him. Hopefully all is well. That is pretty much it. They found your book in his duffle bag on the boat and started trying to find you. When he realized who you were, he took a personal interest in getting you to the hospital."

She sat there with tears streaming down her face. She didn't really know how to feel about Tristan. Apparently he had not told her everything so she wouldn't worry. Or was there some other motive for keeping his secret life from her. Why hadn't she pried more into his personal life, what were they going to do now? *Too many questions and not enough reasonable answers.*

They were driving at a safe fast speed, but it seemed like the miles were just passing by very slowly. She got on her cell phone and called Penny who was about four car lengths behind her. They talked for a short while. Jared was quiet, thinking of what he could do for his friend. After what seemed like an eternity they arrived at the hospital. As she walked into the room, there he laid, quiet, as if he were simply asleep. The heart monitor and other machines were hooked up making their soft humming noises. The nurse was making notes in his chart. She looked up at Julia and saw the hurt in her eyes. She walked over to her and asked if there was anything she needed. Before she could answer, the colonel came in. He introduced himself and asked her to sit down. For the next hour he talked to her about Tristan's condition, the pros and cons of the situation, and his relationship with her father.

"There are special visitor's quarters upstairs on the fifth floor and you are welcome to stay as long as you would like." He said. He left her alone with Tristan. Jared and Penny were in the waiting room talking when the Colonel came out of the room. He gave them the same scenario as he had given Julia, although he didn't go into as much detail with Penny as he had with Julia. Jared knew most of the story already, no need to let any more of it out than need be. Jared apologized for his harshness when they first met, he explained to Penny that he and Tristan had been friends for a long time and he was just concerned about his injuries and recovery possibilities.

A she sat beside the bed, holding his hand, she reminisced about the time they had spent together. She prayed to the Good Lord that he would come out of the coma and be able to speak to her. She had fallen in love with him unconditionally and would be by his side for as long as he wanted her.

"There are so many things I want to tell you my love, I just wish you could hear me." She said. A short while later, the CO came back to the room.

"Here is a key to one of the visitor's rooms upstairs. I have made arrangements for you to stay as long as necessary. Your lady friend can stay also, but I am not sure for how long. There is a cafeteria in the basement of the hospital, and there is a quiet area on the top floor of the building. If you venture out onto the roof, be sure to take your key, as the door will lock behind you. As he left, Penny and Jared were walking into the room. They sat and talked for a long time. Jared had some friends in the area, and he would stay with them for a while. Penny would stay for a couple of days and try to take Julia back to Savannah.

"Absolutely not!" she exclaimed. "I am going to stay here till he wakes up."

"But what if it takes weeks or even months, or maybe never? You have to be realistic bout this, Julia. He may never wake up. You had a wonderful week with this man, but apparently it just wasn't meant to be. You have to get on with your life. You have obligations to yourself and your friends. You just cannot up and leave your place and stay here. Besides it isn't healthy. You don't have any legal ties to this man. You cannot make any decisions for him, you and he were just a fling, you aren't married, hell, you aren't even going steady. You only knew him for a week. Wake up and realize what you are doing here." Penny said.

Julia walked over to the window and stared at the ocean. After a short time she turned around and said.

"I love him, Penny. I love him like I have never loved anyone else before. He has brought a joy to my life that I cannot explain. You can leave anytime you want. When you do I would appreciate if you would look into my cottage when you get there. I will be here until he wakes up no matter how long it takes; end of discussion. You know me well enough that when I make up my mind there is no changing it, and I have made a decision on this. I know he loves me too, and that we were meant to be together. Even if it is like this."

They left the room and Julia sat in the chair next to the bed. She took Tristan's hand and held it for a long time. She finally said, "I am here my darling. I know you may not be able to hear me, but somewhere, somehow, we will be together again. I know you will awake at the proper time, until then I will be by your side."

For the next three days, she had the same routine. She would stay in the room with him almost constantly. Talking to him as if he would hear her and reply. She talked about her book, the time they had spent together, how he had made her feel and the loneliness she had for him after he left. She told him that she understood why he didn't tell her the whole story about his position in the Navy. She told him many stories of how her father had served in the same branch of the service and shared some of her episodes of growing up. She talked about her book and how she was coming along with it. Every so often, he would move, make a grimacing look on his face, or just grunt. She thought he may have opened his eyes at one point, but the nurse explained to her that these were just muscle spasms. She got involved with the physical therapy sessions. Whenever they would come in to give Tristan a treatment, she would watch and learn what to do to keep his muscles from growing stiff. After a while she took over the afternoon sessions exercising his legs and arms and massaging his muscles. Penny would come in the room a couple of times during the day. After the third day, Julia told her that she probably should leave and go back home. There was nothing for her to do there and she had the antique shop to care for back in Savannah. Jared was still under the doctor's care and had transferred his hospital records to the orthopedic department there so he could continue his treatment. The whirlpool made his knee feel a lot better and he was making very good progress. He had graduated from crutches to a cane, and was walking around inside with out the aid of anything. His usual daily routine started early in the morning with physical therapy, laps in the swimming pool, and then back to the whirlpool. He had found a small apartment near the hospital that would take a month-to-month lease; as a matter of fact the owners catered to the families of military personnel who were in the hospital for treatment. It was a small one-bedroom efficiency that was furnished very well for what it was. He had been checking in on Tristan every morning and evening. Whenever he would go into the room, Julia would be there reading to him, or exercising his legs and arms, and rubbing lotion all over his body in order to keep him from getting bedsores. According to the nurses, they would sometimes find her in his room in the middle of the night. Her excuse was that she couldn't sleep and wanted to come down and check on him. Jared tried to talk her into going home and checking on her place, but she refused to leave. She simply told him that Penny would check on her house for her and that she was absolutely not going to leave Tristan there alone. Penny had left her cell phone number with Jared and told him to call her if anything changed. She would be coming back for the weekend soon to check up on Julia. It had been a week since Julia had arrived at the hospital. She had made herself quite at home in the little one bedroom suite upstairs. The entire top floor of the hospital was built with rooms for families of wounded or injured servicemen. She had gotten to know the nurses on a first name basis, and even spent some time in the coffee shop with the CO. He had told her stories of some of the incidents he and her father had gotten into while they were stationed together. Penny had called and told her that she would be coming for a visit this weekend and asked if she wanted anything from the house.

"Do you know where I keep all of my writing materials?" Julia asked.

"I think so," Penny replied. "I'll go to the house and phone you from there, and in the meantime, just make up a list of what you want and I'll bring it."

"Thanks, I'm going to need my laptop and the research materials I have on the desk. Looks like I am going to be here for a while, and I'll work while I am here in his room. Who knows, he might want to listen to what I am composing this time before anyone else gets a chance to read it; and don't forget my two favorite sweaters, it is getting a little cooler in here at night. Also, I sometimes walk in the garden and the night air is cool. Looks like fall will be here a little sooner than I expected and I don't want to be caught off guard."

Penny packed up the items Julia had requested and had made a list while they were talking on the phone. She had checked her messages for her about every other day. The only important ones were from her publisher asking how she was coming on her book. She was under contract and although the process normally takes a few months they wanted to make sure Julia would make the deadline. When she finished talking to Julia she phoned Jared on her way home. She wanted to make sure he was going to be there this weekend. They had been in touch over the phone and she thought he might be interested in her. After all, she wasn't in bad shape, and it had been a long time since she had a meaningful relationship with anyone. She thought maybe she would pursue this a little farther just to see how it would go. He seemed like a pretty good person, and the stories he told of some of the places he had visited intrigued her. She wanted to know more about some of the places he had mentioned. They talked for a short while and he told her that he would be there for the weekend. He was looking forward to seeing her again and hoped that they might go out for dinner or something while she was there.

As she pulled into the garage she almost felt like a schoolgirl again. Tomorrow would be a good day, just how good, she had no idea.

The rays of the early morning sun were just coming through the window. Julia had been to the café downstairs for coffee and had a muffin this morning instead of eggs. As she walked up the stairs to the fourth floor she had a strange feeling. Nothing she could put her finger on, she just thought something would be different today, or at least she hoped it would. As she opened the door to Tristan's room, she noticed a vase of flowers on the table by the window. She walked over to the table and opened the card. It simply said, "Get well soon." The card was written in a man's handwriting, she just assumed that it was from Jared or the commander. As she looked out the window, she noticed that the leaves on thee trees were turning. *Fall of the year, she thought, and my most favorite times. Sweaters, fires in the fireplace, and hometown football games would be just around the corner.*

This also signaled the end of summer and the realization that winter wouldn't be too far away. Many thoughts ran through her mind, but most especially ones of what lie ahead for she and Tristan. She looked at him sleeping peacefully. She knelt beside his bed and said her early morning prayers. Although she prayed all day at one time or another, she especially prayed in the morning and in the evening. She walked down the stairs and out into the courtyard. For some strange reason she was drawn to the outside this morning. The sun was bright and the early morning breeze rustled her hair. Her thoughts drifted back to the seven days in Savannah that she and Tristan had spent together when they first met. The wonderful times they had exploring the city and each other. The fun days in the parks and the steamy nights at her little cottage. He had touched her in places she never knew she had. A warm feeling came over her each time she thought about him. She could almost feel his naked body close to hers, his arms wrapped around her, kissing her softly on the back of her neck and downward. As she slowly walked along the path she thought about the first night they met, how she almost didn't say anything to him, but let her heart override her gut feelings.

The silence of the garden was overcome by the noise of the F 16's flying overhead. All of a sudden she was snapped back to reality. She needed to finish the walk and get back to Tristan.

Jared Olson finished his session in the whirlpool and headed for the showers. He was expecting Penny sometime this afternoon and they tentatively had a dinner date set up for tonight. As he showered, he thought of how she looked the last time he saw her. For someone who was four years older than he, she still looked good. She apparently took very good care of herself. She still had it in all the right places; that is unless there was something holding them up. He finished dressing and headed to Tristan's room to check on him. When he got there, nothing had changed; he was still hooked up to the machines, sleeping as if he were just resting. Blood pressure and heart rhythms were normal, and all seemed well. As he left the room, the commander approached him in the hallway. "Letter for you, son."

"Thank you sir, " he replied.

As he got on the elevator, he opened the letter. It merely stated that they wanted him to come back for a briefing on a new assignment. He was somewhat perplexed at this. Here he was, still on medical leave, and they wanted him to return for a meeting about another assignment? That didn't make any sense. Oh well, he would call the commander in Fort Oglethorpe and find out what was going on. As he got off the elevator, his cell phone rang.

"Are we still on for dinner?" Penny asked.

"Sure thing, when will you be here?" he asked.

"About fifteen minutes. Want to meet me at the hospital, since I don't know where your apartment is?"

They had talked on the phone a couple of times and he had told her that he had a month-to-month lease on a small apartment while he was staying in town.

"Sure thing, I just need to go home and change clothes." He replied.

"OK, I'll meet you at the hospital. I have some things for Julia that she asked me to bring.

Julia had just finished her exercise regiment with Tristan; there was still no sign of his waking up.

He just lay there as if he was asleep. Occasionally he would move his arms or legs, but the nurses said that those were just muscle spasms. Julia didn't believe that. She kept telling herself that he would wake up and they would be together again. She would keep talking to him, reading him stories from newspapers, books, and just about anything that he might like. They had several conversations during their week together, but they didn't talk much about hobbies. He was fascinated with Savannah and the surroundings, and didn't talk much about himself. She had so much she wanted to ask him. *She wanted to know every detail he could tell her about his past life, but would she ever get the chance?*

Penny came through the door like a bull in a china shop, dropping stuff off the pushcart, and knocking over anything that got in her way.

"Where did the flowers come from?" she asked.

"Not sure, haven't really had time to try to find out." She replied as she got up from the chair and gave Penny a welcome hug.

"Things are pretty much the same at home, I go by the house a couple of times a week and everything still is pretty much the way you left it. I even stopped and talked to the nosy old lady that lives next door and she said that no one had been around. She asked about you and I just told her that you were away doing some research on materials you needed for your next book. She apparently believed me because she didn't ask anymore questions."

"Thanks, girl, I owe you one."

"How's he doing?" Penny asked.

"Things haven't changed much since the last time you were here." Julia replied.

"He has been a little more restless for the last couple of days. I would have sworn that he was trying to open his eyes this morning, but the nurses just passed it off to muscle spasms. I have had some pretty peculiar feelings today, can't put my finger on it, but something is definitely changing. He has broken out in night sweats a couple of times, and turns his head like he is having a nightmare."

"You are just hoping, Julia. You must face the facts. He hasn't been awake since before you came here, and there is a chance that he may never wake up. I know you say you love him, but you may never get the chance to really do that. You have got to be realistic about all of this. If I were you I would be making preparations for the worst and hope for the best."

She unloaded the cart and put the box of materials and her laptop over in the corner by the window. As she walked towards the door, she asked.

"Want to go to dinner with Jared and I?"

"No thanks, I'll just stay here. You guys haven't seen each other in a while, and I think you like him and maybe it would be good for you to find someone. You cannot ever tell when or where it will happen, just hang in there. I'll be here reading to him for most of the evening. Go on and have a good time. I am in the same room; just let yourself in if I am not there.

They gave your room to someone else and there is an extra bed in mine just in case."

About that time Jared appeared at the door and Penny's eyes seemed to brighten up a couple of notches. They waved good-bye and off they went. When they got to the elevator he gave her a long awaited kiss. As their tongues met, she felt an electrical sensation all through her body. This guy was a very good kisser. The door opened and as they stepped in a feeling of ecstasy came over her. Sure she had been with a couple of men since her divorce, but they didn't make her feel the way Jared did. There was just something commanding about him. She liked the way he took the lead in each situation. They had talked several times on the phone and when she had left the last time the way he kissed her made her want to come back even more.

"Where would you like to go," he asked.

"Not really sure, have any suggestions?" she replied.

"I have a taste for something different. I have been eating my own cooking for quite some time now, and I really would like to have Mexican or Chinese for a change. You can only eat sandwiches, bacon and eggs, waffles, or cold cereal so much," he laughed.

"I am in an oriental mood myself, how about Chinese?"

"Ok, there is a small restaurant about ten minutes from here. Let's give it a try. I have been there only once, but it was good then."

"Sounds great, then Chinese it is." She replied. She tossed him the keys to her SUV and away they went. As they pulled out of the parking lot, he looked over at her and smiled.

The evening rays of the sun had given way to the sparkling of the stars. Julia had brought another book from her collection to read to Tristan. She had gotten through the first chapter and drifted off to sleep. He seemed restless earlier, and she wondered if he had begun to respond to her reading and talking to him.

*A loud thunderous noise went off in his head, and a blinding flash of light followed. He had a tremendous headache. His eyes were closed as they had been for quite some time now. As he tried to clear his mind, he sensed that someone was near him. His sense of smell wanted him to believe that Julia was there, but he had no knowledge of where he was. But where was he? As the grogginess in his mind began to disappear, he tried to open his eyes. He sensed that they were open, but there was nothing but darkness. He started making mental notes about his condition. **"I can feel my legs, my arms, and wiggle my fingers and toes, but I cannot see anything, am I blind, or just have something wrapped around my head?".** He tried to feel his head, but his hand was restrained. His other hand was strapped in also. **"Ok, where am I?" he thought. " It smells like a hospital in here, but what hospital could it be?"** He tried to slow his breathing down and get it under control. The last thing he remembered was jumping from the helicopter and seeing the missile just before he hit the water. After that there was a loud noise and a bright burst of light with a deafening sound in his ears. Where are the others? How long had he been out? Had the mission been accomplished? So much he wanted to know.* He bit down hard on the breathing tube and tasted the lousy taste of plastic. He had only experienced this taste once before, and that was when he had to have his appendix removed. The smell of the operating room and the taste of the plastic in his mouth were two things he didn't want to experience again. Just as he was drifting back to sleep, he felt someone wiping his forehead with a soft cloth. He moved the fingers on both hands and tried to make someone aware that he was awake. At first Julia couldn't believe her eyes. She went to the door and screamed for the nurse. She could have just pushed the button, but under the circumstances, she thought it would be faster to find her personally.

The head nurse came in and had the others call for the doctor in charge of that shift. His chart had been noted that as soon as he regained consciousness the commander had to be notified. When the doctor entered the room, he asked Julia to leave. "Not on your life, you'll have to have me carried out of here kicking and screaming before I'll let that happen. I have been waiting on this for weeks, and I am not about to leave now!" About that time the commander entered the room and heard most of the conversation.

"Let her stay, " he told the others.

"Julia, you will have to stay over there out of the way while they work on him. He may be able to speak, and maybe not. Let's have a positive attitude about this and work with it in whatever stages it takes."

She agreed and stood over near the window. They removed the bandages from his eyes and the breathing tube from his throat. His vital signs were stable, and his heart rhythm and pulse were stable also. The doctor told him not to try to speak, just simply nod his head if he understood. A simple yes and no would be sufficient right now. As they removed the straps from his arms and hands that held them to the rails he raised his right hand. The doctor said to hold up two fingers for yes and one finger for no. Asked if he understood, he held up two fingers. They darkened the room as much as they could, and took the bandages off his face. He slowly opened his eyes and squinted, as the light seemed to filter in. For the first few moments he had trouble focusing. His head felt like someone was pounding him with a mallet. Julia stood motionless, tears streaming down her face. She had prayed earnestly for this moment. She had already made up her mind that she was going to stay by his side until he awoke. No matter how long it took. She silently thanked God for letting him awake. The doctor informed Julia that they would be taking him upstairs to the intensive care unit, just to keep a closer watch on his vital signs. They would call back later and let her know how he was doing and when she could come up and visit with him. The commander told her just to sit tight; he would make sure that Tristan knew that she was there. Just as they moved the bed towards the door everything finally came into focus. He looked over at Julia and gave her a soft smile. At first, he thought that he was dreaming again, but he knew that she was real and not just a figment of his imagination. She walked over to the bed, leaned over and gave him a soft kiss on the forehead "I love you," she simply said. He responded by holding up two fingers and forcing a smile. She spent the rest of the night walking the floor, stopping ever so often to look out the window and thank God for bringing him around.

Sometime around 2 a.m. she sat down in the sofa sleeper and nodded off to sleep. She had tried to call Penny but neither her phone nor Jared's would answer. Each went directly to voice mail. As she drifted off to sleep, she had visions of what the future would hold for them. The commander had told her the whole story, although he had left out most of the details. There would be some things that Tristan would have to fill in, that is, if he would. It didn't matter; all that mattered now was that he had woken up and recognized her. All during the time she had spent in the hospital room, she had expected the worst and hoped for the best. She had checked on the Internet in regards to concussions and their effects on the human brain. There had been wide speculations from both ends of the spectrums. It went everywhere from small headache to being blind and deaf for the rest of their lives. She had already made up her mind that no matter what, *she would stay by his side for as long as he would have her*. And that also was something she had worried about, *would he still want her, or had she just been someone who had just passed through his life?*

Shortly after dawn the commander came into the room and woke her up. He sat on the ottoman in front of the chair and explained the situation to her.

"They are running a battery of tests on him. He will be in and out of reality for a couple of days. Apparently his vital signs are as close to normal as they can be. He has uttered a few words in a whisper tone. He has asked to see you and I told him that as soon as he was capable that you would be the first one to get to see him. At that he smiled. Just bear with them until they get him comfortable and under control. He has a terrible headache and it is probably from the swelling in his brain. They may have to do surgery to relieve the pressure, but not until they have exhausted every other method. They are in the process of doing a brain scan at the present time. Why don't you go upstairs to your room and they will call you as soon as they have something to tell you?"

She sat there with tears streaming down her face. She barely understood what he was saying. All kinds of things were running through her mind. "Do you have any idea how long it will take? I really would like to see him, and I know he wants to see me. Please sir, help me as much as you can." She pleaded.

"I'll see what I can do. I cannot make any promises, but I will get you in as soon as possible. There are some other people who want to talk to him also, I am sure you have to know what they want. I will caution you in this, don't ask him any questions about the mission. It was under the highest security and somehow it got breached. No one was supposed to know they were coming, and apparently they did. You just don't get that lucky. They were flying under radar so close to the water you could feel the spray from the rotors of the helicopter. Get some rest, I'll call you as soon as I know something."

She thanked him and sat there for a few minutes with her head in her hands. *What would happen now? How would he react to her being there? How long would he have to stay?* Many thoughts ran through her mind. She settled down into the bed. She simply pulled the covers over her as she had been very tired and had not slept much all night. The few catnaps she had during the night hadn't helped much, but her feeling was correct. She had known that something was about to happen, she just didn't know what. It could have been very bad, but it seemed like it turned out to be very good. As she drifted off to sleep, she envisioned them in the hammock out on the dock at evening tide, enjoying Tybee Time.

The restaurant was fairly full by the time they had arrived. Although it seemed very busy, there were several parking places close to the building. Jared was thankful for this, as even though he had been taking physical therapy three days per week, it still pained him a little to have to walk very long distances. As they walked in the entrance, the smell of the fresh food was tantalizing. They had lettuce wraps for appetizers and the lemon pepper chicken and honey shrimp dishes for dinner didn't last very long. They started out with a single glass of Riesling and before dinner was over, they had consumed a whole bottle.

"Where are you staying while you are in town?" he asked as they left.

"I guess I will just bunk in with Julia at the hospital. Haven't really given it much thought. "

Want to stop by the house for a night cap?" he asked.

"It isn't very far from here, and it is clean, I have spent the last couple of days straightening up in anticipation of seeing you while you were here."

"Sure, why not?" she replied. She was hoping that he would ask her up to his apartment. She could hardly wait to have him kiss her again. She almost melted into his arms at the hospital and was eager to find out if kissing was the only thing he did well.

"I'll pick up my truck later when I take you to the hospital. If that is ok." He said.

Fine she thought, that would be more time she could spend with him alone and not have to share him or his time with anyone else.

She checked her cell phone and there were no messages. A couple of missed calls from Danielle Bellefonte but she was sure that they could wait till morning. She hadn't had anything interesting to talk about for the last couple of days. She had met a young sailor at one of the bars in town and liked him quite a bit. They had spent some time together, but decided not to have anything else to do with him after he told her that he was gay and just wanted a good looking woman to accompany him while he was waiting to leave town in a few days.

For a furnished efficiency the apartment was very tastefully decorated. The darker colors added to the masculinity of the space. She was expecting to see a small one-room apartment with an air-conditioned/heater combo sticking out of the window. As they pulled into the driveway, she realized that it was actually an apartment built on top of a two-car garage. As they walked up the stairs, a couple of squirrels ran across the porch railing each with a peanut in its mouth. "Pet's I assume?" she asked as he unlocked the door.

"Just a couple of vagabonds that have been terrorizing the neighborhood. I got acquainted with them shortly after I moved in. Apparently the previous tenants must have fed them quite a bit, as they are almost tame. They sometimes sit in the windowsill and watch me as I eat dinner. Most of the time I have to go into the living room just to keep from feeling sorry for them. I almost have them eating out of my hand, would like to try it sometime just to see if I could. *That shouldn't be too hard to do, she thought.*

He turned on the television and asked if she would like a drink.

"Sure, if you are going to have one also." She replied.

He sat down on the sofa beside her. They watched the television is silence for a few minutes and she asked, "How long before you have to go back to doing whatever it is you have to do?"

"Don't know, I am on medical leave until the doctor releases me."

"Just what is it that you do in the service, and what branch of it are you in.?"

"I am in the Naval Reserve,'" he replied.

"I work on communications equipment in large ships. Sometimes when the captain's stereo goes out, the call for me to come in and fix it." He said with a laugh.

He was lying out of his ass, but there was no way that he was going to tell her that he and Tristan were members of the number two seal team in the world; and that they had been decorated three times for service above and beyond, and that they had traveled all over the globe together.

"She slapped him on the arm, and said "Ok that was funny, now tell me what you really do."

"He simply smiled and told her that he was a communications officer and that he specialized in world wide radio transmissions to troops all over the country.

"Like Good Morning Viet Nam?" she asked.

"No silly, I work on different radio communications all over the world. The government sends me to school once every year to learn the latest technology in radio waves." That was the closest that he could come to with out coming out and telling her that he eavesdropped on nearly every country in the world and could speak half of the different languages also.

"Now what is it that you do?" he said as he turned to face her on the sofa.

"I own a small antique store in Savannah. I bought it with the proceeds from my divorce. My husband was more interested in playing around with other women than taking care of me. Unfortunately for him and fortunate for me, he came from one of the richest families in the state, and made a very nice settlement with me out of court. He was supposedly a southern gentleman and we settled out of court for an undisclosed amount of money just so I wouldn't tell the scandals in the newspapers. I made some smart investments with some of the cash, and have a pretty nice nest egg for myself.

"Pretty smart," he replied. "Most women would have gone on a spending spree and wouldn't have half of the money left.

"Have you ever been married?" she asked.

"Nope, not that I don't like the idea, but I just haven't settled down long enough to find the right one. My travels take me to different corners of the world and I never know really how long I will be gone at any one time."

"Do you ever get tired of the traveling?" she asked.

"Not really, I have seen just about every continent in the world, I mean there are still some places that I would like to visit on a civilian basis, but it would have to be under different circumstances. Who knows, maybe someday I'll strike it rich and travel all over the world?"

He sat his wine glass down on the sofa table and as he turned he could see the sparkle in her green eyes. He lowered his lips to hers and kissed her for what seemed like an eternity. She closed her eyes and thought of nothing but the fireworks that were going off all over. The butterflies in her stomach as stopped fluttering and she was comfortable in his arms. After another couple of glasses she asked where the bathroom was. He pointed to the bedroom and said, "it is to the left of the bed."

While she was gone he opened the refrigerator door and took out another bottle of wine.

A short while later, he walked into the bedroom to make sure she was all right. As he opened the door there she lay, almost naked, under the covers.

"I thought you might need a damsel in distress to rescue," she said. With that, he calmly set the bottle and the glasses on the bedside table and as he turned around, he noticed she had one of his tee shirts on. She stood on the bed on her knees and helped him unbutton his shirt and trousers. He climbed into bed and as he snuggled close, she kissed him again. For the next few hours, they knew no one else was around. They made love into the wee hours of the morning. One time during the night he awoke to her staring at him. "Something wrong?" he asked.

"No, not really," she replied.

"I know you might find this hard to believe, but I just don't jump into bed with every man that takes me out to supper." She said.

"The thought never crossed my mind, either you are one hell of an actor, or you haven't been this close to a man in quite a while. Most of the time men can tell, just like women can. I don't make rash judgments, Penny. It doesn't make for good friendships or companionship. I simply feel that we are put on this earth to enjoy everything that the Good Lord has given us. If He made anything better than this, He would have kept it for himself." He rolled over and curled his arms around her. They fell asleep and not until the phone rang did they know what was going on outside of their little world.

Julia awoke a couple of hours later to the sound of someone opening the door. As Penny walked into the room, she asked about Tristan. Julia gave her the good news, that he had awoken sometime during the night and they took him upstairs to the intensive care unit in order to monitor his actions. After being in a coma for as long as he was, they wanted to make sure that he was not injured somewhere else. Also, the headaches he was complaining about were brought on by the swelling in his brain and they needed to monitor that also. They sat and talked for a long time. Eventually Penny told her all about last night. She told her about how gentle Jared was and how he made her feel like no one else have ever made her feel. She had not checked her messages on her cell phone, or she would have already known this. Apparently Jared hadn't checked his, or he would have already called. Penny tried to call him on his phone but it still was going to voice mail. They sat for a while longer and there came a knock on Julia's door. As she opened it the commander stepped inside.

"He is doing just fine," he said. "They are doing an MRI on him to make sure there aren't any broken bones that cannot be seen by x-rays. They think the swelling in his brain will go down and if it doesn't they may have to do surgery to relieve the pressure. They want to give it another couple of days."

"When can I see him/'she asked.

"He is sleeping now, I have instructed the nurse to call here and let you know when he wakes up. You should be able to get in to see him soon."

"Has he asked anything about me, or ......?"

"Yes," he replied. "He has said that he wants to see you as soon as possible; but remember, he has been through quite a traumatic event. He may be drifting in and out of consciousness. He is asking some pretty off the wall questions, so don't be alarmed.

I'll check in on him myself later. You have my number, if there is anything else you need, just let me know." he said.

Julia had gotten up to listen to what he had to say, and just as he turned to walk out the door, she gave him a hug and with tears in her eyes, simply said "Thank You Sir."

She turned around and started towards the bathroom. "Maybe a shower will wash away some of the anxieties." She told Penny.

"It sure worked wonders for me this morning." Penny answered.

"How long are you planning to stay this time," Julia asked.

"Not really sure, Jared has to leave in a couple of days for some sort of meeting back at the base and I probably need to get myself back to the store. I'll stay as long as necessary if you need me for something."

"It's not really that, I wish I had said something to you before you came. I need my car. I have been stuck around here since we came and fortunately didn't need to go anywhere, but as soon as he is ready to go, I would like to take him home with me so I can look after him." Julia said.

"Aren't you jumping the gun a little bit?" Penny asked. "How do you know he will want to go home with you? He may have a home of his own that he needs to take care of, or better still, he may have some family that wants to take care of him. Don't set yourself up for another disappointment. Just let things happen as they may. Ask him what he wants to do before you start making plans."

"Maybe you are right," Julia replied. "Although he told me he wanted me to wait for him and that he couldn't wait to get back to see me, I really don't know much about him at all. He said he had a friend here in Jacksonville but I find it strange that no one has contacted him about this. There must be something terribly wrong. I am sure they talk to each other as Tristan once told me that his friend was keeping his motorcycle for him. With all of this HIPA stuff I know they aren't going to give me any information on him. You are probably right, maybe I should just wait, if worse comes to worse, I'll just rent a car, drive it home, and get mine and drive back; maybe that is the best thing to do anyway."

Just about that time, the telephone rang and it was the ICU nurse calling to tell her that he was awake and wanting to see her.

She ran a brush through her hair, dabbed on a little makeup, and out the door she went.

"You may want to keep trying to get Jared, as I am sure he will want to see him as soon as he can, that is if you guys can tear yourselves away from each other." Before she could answer, the door was closed and Julia was almost running down the hallway towards the elevators. As she punched the button for the third floor, the elevator seemed to be moving at a snail's pace. When the doors opened into the unit, she noticed that everyone was wearing hospital garb. They met her as she came to the nurse's station. "Are Julia?" the nurse asked.

"Yes, why?"

"Just wanted to make sure. Not too many people are allowed to see this patient. Put this mask and gown on and follow me. He has been asking for you ever since he woke up. We have managed to get some real food down him, but he keeps mumbling something about" Special Lemonade."

Julia just smiled; sounded like he was getting his sense of humor back. As she approached the bed, he was propped up on a pillow and was fully awake. She simply bent over the rail and kissed him softly on the lips.

"Welcome back" she said with a smile.

"I was really looking forward to seeing you again, but not like this."

"I know, but better than not at all; isn't it?" he said.

"We will take it one day at a time," she said.

"It really doesn't matter how long it takes, we just want to get you well."

"That's right, I have had a lot of time to think, and I am ready to stop traveling all over the world. Julia, you have brought happiness to my life that I have never experienced, and I want to spend as much time with you as I can. I love you. It may take a while, but we will get there, I know it."

"I love you too, and no matter how long it takes, we will work it out. I am just happy that you are back safe and ok."

They talked for a long time. He relayed to her that the doctors were going to keep him there for a few days for observation and that his commanders would have to come in and get his side of the story of what happened and tell him what he didn't know. He also told her that he didn't tell her the complete truth about what part of the service he was in because he didn't want her to worry about him while he was gone. Plus, he could only tell her so much. He didn't really know where he was going when he boarded the ship, he just knew that it involved his team and that it had to be something really important to national security in order for them to be activated again. The tests were to start tomorrow morning and the investigators would be there in the next few days. He should be able to be discharged within a week if nothing serious was found. Eventually he would have to travel to Virginia to headquarters for some more debriefing, but that could come later. They knew how to get in touch with him, and would do so at the necessary time.

"Could you come and stay with me to recuperate?" she asked. "And would you want to?"

"I don't see why not, they really don't care where I am as long as they know where they can reach me," he replied.

"And they have never failed to find me when they wanted me.

I have a couple of weeks of physical therapy and who knows what else, so I am not going to be leaving here anytime soon."

With that they decided Julia would go back to Savannah and make preparations for him to stay with her; at least until he was completely recuperated. She gave him a kiss and told him that she would stop by to say goodbye on her way out. As she walked out the door, he watched her until she was completely out of sight. Even in baggy sweat pants and a sweatshirt, she was still as beautiful as ever. *Thank you Lord for bringing us together, he silently prayed. You know I have asked you for quite some time now for someone to love and be happy with. I sure hope she is the one. The only thing I didn't see, Lord, was the wings; when do you put them on?*

When Julia reached the room that had been her home for the better part of two weeks, Penny was nowhere to be found. She had left her a note that she and Jared were going for a ride and they could be reached on her cell phone. Although she couldn't get them to answer, she was already making plans. She would ride back to Savannah with Penny, start cleaning up the old home place where her parents lived, and welcome Tristan home to a good old fashioned down home hospitality. Jared could ride back with them and catch a flight back when he needed to come back to Jacksonville. There were a lot of things to do, but they would get them done. She hadn't stayed in the old home place because it was just too big for her. The old two story antebellum at the end of Forsythe Street on Tybee Island held many fond memories of family togetherness. Maybe, just maybe, it could do it again. She called her neighbor, Mrs. Perkins and told her of her plan. Of course she knew nothing of Tristan, but was sure if that is what Julia thought was right, then she would help her get it done. They would take the covers off the furniture and have the house cleaned in a couple of days. Penny finally called her back and Julia told her of the plans.

"I think that is a great idea, Jared has been wanting to visit Savannah ever since we met, and this will give him a chance to really see it like he should. I'll talk it over with him and call you back." It didn't take Penny long to convince Jared to make the trip, she even offered to drive him back in case he didn't want to fly. They were on the way back to the hospital to try and visit with Tristan before they left. Jared had not gotten a chance to see his favorite C O and he wasn't about to leave without talking to him. He let Penny off the elevator and proceeded to the third floor. The "guardian" met him at the nurse's station and wasn't about to let him past her. When she refused to let Jared by, he called the commander.

"I have been waiting to hear from you Jared, I knew you would be around soon." He said. "Not soon enough, though. How about telling Atilla the Hun that it is ok for me to see Tristan. I've shown her my credentials, but she said she could make up something like that from her computer if she wanted to, not to mention that she thought I was a smart ass!"

"Well, son, you sometimes come on a little strong. Especially if you aren't in good mood. I understand your feeling bad about almost losing your entire team, but don't take it out on everyone. They aren't the enemy, we will find out who is responsible for this, I promise."

With that he handed the phone to the nurse and she reluctantly let him pass, but only with a growl.

Tristan was about half asleep when Jared walked into the room. "Hey Boss," he said, "that was one hell of a way to extend your vacation."

Tristan opened his eyes and gave him a sad smile.

"You know the others didn't make, don't you?" he said.

"Yes sir," he replied. "I got the story from the commander the day I arrived. Sorry about Big Jim and the rest of the guys, we had been through a lot together. He had just told me, not more than two weeks ago, about the ranch he had bought and how he was thinking about retiring and planning on spending the rest of his time with his wife and kids. He had just got the youngest out of college and was looking forward to some fun times with Emily."

"I know, that is the hard part, but the hardest part was me not being able to be there for the funerals. I hope the girls understood."

"I am sure they did, they asked about you and I told them that you were in a hospital somewhere because you were still unconscious from the blast and hadn't woken up yet.

There were lots of dignitaries there, hell even the "General" came. He usually doesn't attend these things, most of the time he just sends his regards with someone." Jared said.

"I know, it isn't like him to take this much of an interest in something like this. Must be more to it than we know about. How's the leg? Big Jim told me about the injury, haven't I told you that you would probably get hurt worse on that damned motorcycle than you would on a mission?"

"Yes sir, you did, but I remember someone who dumped theirs right in front of his friends' house not too far from here. By the way, how is Tad doing? I haven't heard anything from him and I kind of suspected that he might be here. Seeing's how you are in his home town and all."

"I haven't called him yet. He told me when I left that he had a funny feeling about this one, and that I should be really careful. Does Julia know about him? " He asked.

"No, all she knows is that I have a close friend here, she doesn't know he is that close or that he lives in the same town. Speaking of her, I am going to be staying for a little while in Savannah while I am recuperating. I am thinking about hanging it up, Jared. We have been all over the world more than once, and it is about time to let someone else do the dirty work. We lost five of our best friends this time, and it is pure fate that we aren't laying beside them. Anyway, don't let the cat out of the bag just yet. I still have a lot of decisions to make about my life. Julia is a wonderful person and I am going to enjoy spending some time with her. Hell, I might even ask her to marry me."

"Damn, you did take a big hit to the brain talking like that. I have two more weeks of therapy and they are already telling me that I will have to go back to Langley for some special assignment. Couldn't think what the hell it could be, now that I don't have a regular team to go out with. I didn't think they reassigned you this quick; do you think something is wrong?" He asked.

"Couldn't tell you, my promotion was a big surprise to me. Especially with someone as important as the General coming out to talk to me about it. The commander here at the naval hospital has already told me that they are sending people out here as soon as I am up to all of the questioning. Who knows what will happen. Let's just stay in touch and let the chips fall where they may. Do you still have the same cell number?"

"Yes sir, and I haven't given it to very many people. Just my dad, my other family members, and one girl. Penny Oglethorpe."

"So you have met Penny Oglethorpe, huh?"

"Why do you ask that, sir?" he asked.

"Don't sir me and you know why I asked you that, don't you?"

"No, not really," he replied.

"Penny Oglethorpe had one of the most vivid imaginations that I have ever seen, not to mention being the nosiest one woman I have ever met."

"You are definitely right about the imagination, she has taught me things I didn't know, and I have been around the world three times and have visited just abut every female nationality know to man! "They both laughed for a few minutes and then Jared told Tristan that he would be taking Julia and Penny back to Savannah and staying a couple of days there. Tristan told him that he would tell him what happened later, he just didn't want to talk about it right now. Besides, he was tired and needed some rest before the physical therapist came in to work on him.

Julia knocked on the commander's office door. As he opened it, he asked her to step inside. The room was very comfortably furnished. Not you're regular run of the mill commanding officer's office. There were dark mahogany bookshelves on both sides of the window behind his desk, and there was a gas fireplace over in the corner, with a very comfortable old wingback chair sitting in front of it. As he sat down, he handed her a copy of one of her books.\ "Would you do me the honor, Ms Deveraux?" he asked.

"Yes sir, I would be honored. I didn't know you were a fan. Why didn't you say something when I first came in?" she asked.

"Because I figured, or at least I had hoped, that I would get a chance to ask you before you left." He replied.

"I have read them all, and am waiting for the next one to come out. I saw your laptop in Tristan's room, but I am assuming that you didn't get much writing in before he came to, did you?"

"No sir," she replied "but there is plenty of time for that later. I am going home to make room for him in the old home place. He has asked to come back to Savannah to recuperate and I am going to play nurse maid."

"I figured as much. You know, watching you for these last few days almost makes me think that you may have missed your calling. The way you took care of him in the room couldn't have been done any better by anyone on my staff here; doctor or nurse."

"I love him sir, I cannot begin to explain how it happened, but I know I love him. And I know he loves me too. I will take care of him for as long as he will let me." She said.

"Any long term plans being made?" he asked.

"Not sure, but when I find out you will be the first to know." she said with a smile.

"I just wanted to tell you how much I appreciate all of the help and special treatment that you gave me. We will never forget it, I can assure you of that."

"Just keep me up to date on you guys, and if anything comes up, such as any kind of special occasion, please let me know. Here is my home address and phone number, you can get me there most anytime I am not here."

With that she stood up and as he came around the desk she stretched out her hand. He took it in his and pulled her close and gave her a hug.

"Richard and Mary Ann would have been very proud of you. I am sure they are smiling down at you right now." He said with a smile.

"Someday you must tell me how you knew them," she asked.

"I will," he replied. "But now is not the time nor the place. Good luck to you and Tristan, and call me sometime."

With that he opened the door and she walked down the hall towards the elevator. As the doors opened she turned and looked back. He had disappeared back into the world of the unknown. But one thing was for sure; he ran one hell of a hospital.

The drive back to Savannah was filled with lots of conversation, but most of it was between Jared and Penny. Where would he stay while he was there? There must be a little motel or boarding house near them. Julia suggested that he stay in her cottage as she would be sleeping and working in the old home place most of the time. He could use the old Chevy for transportation as she was going to get her new car out of the basement and have it ready when she went to get Tristan, that is if he didn't have other transportation. She had taken part of the money that was left to her by her parents and bought herself an SUV. She had plans of doing some traveling and although she had not plotted a destination, she thought at some point in her life she would need it. She had taken the balance of the money and bought out her brother's half interest in the home there on Tybee Island. He had moved away years ago and wasn't fond of being there anyway. He had told her that she could have the place, but she wouldn't think of it. She was stubborn and wanted to make sure that everything was on the up and up so she just had the place appraised and sent him a cashiers check with the proper documents to sign over his interest in the property and was done with it. They weren't very close and since their parents had died she had only seen him twice. They dropped her off at the house and after making sure she was safe, they headed out to the cottage. They passed Danielle Bellefonte on the road in her flashy sports car and she just simply gave them a wave and took off.

"One of these days they will find her off in the river or turned over in the sand the way she drives that damned car." Penny said.

"Is she a wild and dangerous woman?" Jared asked.

"Yes she is, in more ways than one. She is notorious with men. That is why she has been married three times." Penny said.

"So what does your friend do for a living?"

"Nothing, she just marries rich or powerful men and then gets alimony from them. Her first husband died of a heat attack, her second was killed in a plane crash, and the third one she just divorced." Penny replied.

"She has been a busy girl, she doesn't look a day over forty, maybe forty five." Jared remarked.

"She is forty-eight and don't you be getting any ideas. She will try anything, or if you are interested, I can hook you two up."

Jared sensed a hint of jealously and didn't say much for a few minutes. Shortly before they made the turn into the dirt road that led to the cottage, he said, "Look, I was just making conversation, don't get your panties all in a wad. She just looked like someone who might just be crazy and I didn't know if you two were friends or not. I don't really care. Women like her a dime a dozen, I have seen her kind all over the world."

"Well," Penny said, "just what is your kind of woman. Have you ever been married or are you just the adventurous playboy that travels around the world screwing whomever you can get to jump into the sack with you?"

Jared pulled the car over to the side of the road and jammed the gear into park. He sat there for a moment and simply said.

"What I have done in my past, at this point, in none of your damned business. I thought you might be someone who would like to have some fun and build somewhat of a relationship with. Obviously you are mad at all of the men who you come in contact with and just want to secretly make their lives miserable. You can take this car, Savannah, and all that goes with it and stuff it, lady, I don't need this jealously crap and I don't intend to take it from you either."

With that he opened the door, took his duffle bag out of the back seat, and started walking down the road. Penny just sat there for a minute. She had never said anything like that to anyone before, and no one had ever talked back to her that way. He sure had spunk, not to mention that he was great in bed, and a great conversationalist. She got over into the driver's seat and turned the car around. As she slowly approached him walking down the road she rolled the window down and said, "I am sorry can we talk some more? I didn't mean to hurt your feelings, I just an very leery about men, the way I have been treated by my ex-husband and with Danielle I just had a flashback of some old ghosts."

Jared stopped walking and turned toward the car. As he approached the driver's side, he sat the duffle bag down on the road and leaned over into the window.

"I have never been married. I lived with a woman for three years one time and just about the time that I thought everything was going good and was about to ask her to marry me, she went crazy. I never cheated on her; even tough I was in some far away place that I knew she would never find out about it, I never did it. You are going to have to quit wallowing in that ex-husband crap and get on with your life. Not every man in this world is a womanizer, and is on the prowl. If you are going to be like this, you can put the car in drive and keep going. I can find a way back to the airport, get a rental car, and find my way back to Jacksonville. I don't need this shit and I am not going to put up with it. I enjoyed being with you and have had a very good time up till now, so you make the decision as to how you are going to act, and then let me know. I will walk the rest of the way to Julia's cottage, get the key out of the flower box, and let myself in. I am not sure that you and I are going to be good together, so just give me some time to think it over and I'll call you later. If that isn't ok with you then just keep driving and maybe we will see each other sometime."

With that he picked up the duffle bag and started walking. It was only about a half a mile to Julia's cottage, but his knee was already telling him that he shouldn't have let his ego get in the way of the ride, but something had to be done. By the time he reached the cottage he was ready to sit down. After a few minutes he found the key, opened the door, and set his bag on the sofa. He opened the refrigerator door and found a soft drink and as he walked out onto the back porch, he thought of Tristan and how he was apparently in love with Julia.

Why does it have to be so damned hard? Does every woman in the world think that you are trolling all of the time? Why can't I find someone who is trusting and doesn't have a lot of baggage? Maybe I just need to leave her alone, go back to Jacksonville, get my truck and just drive to Langley and forget about the whole damned thing.

As he walked out to the end of the boardwalk, there sat the hammock at the end of the dock. He sat down and let the gentle breeze blow through his thoughts. Pricilla had been the love of his life for three years. They had much fun, traveled a lot, and spent many a night talking about what a future they would have together once Jared decided to resign his position and settle down. Everything was going fine until he surprised her one night coming back from a mission two days early. He sat the roses and the card on the swing on the front porch and walked around the side of the house. She always slept with the window open in the bedroom. Just as he expected, the vehicle that was parked in the front of the neighbor's house wasn't visiting them. The scene that unfolded wasn't what he had imagined coming home to. He went around to the back door, kicked it open and as he opened the bedroom door they both sat up scared as hell. He pointed the pistol at the deliveryman first, and then thought about what he was about to do. All of this time he had loved her, taken care of her, and made some really important plans for them. He simply said, "both of you get your asses out of my house and don't come back."

She stood up crying and tried to talk to him. "Stay away from me!!" he said.

"I am leaving. I will be back day after tomorrow, if you don't have all of your stuff out of here by then, I'll haul it off myself! I loved you and trusted you with everything I had, I cannot believe you would treat me like this."

With that he walked out the front door and as her lover sped away he fired three rounds up into the air as if to let him know what he almost got himself into. He took the roses and threw them out into the yard, and got into his vehicle and drove off. The next place he stopped was his favorite watering hole. He sat there for the next three hours and tried to drown away his sorrows. At closing time, Jon the bartender simply took him into the back room and laid him on the couch in the office. His apartment was upstairs over the bar and he had taken Jared's keys with him to make sure he didn't wake up sometime during the night and try to drive. Hell, he couldn't walk much less drive a damned car.

Jon woke him up the next morning and he vowed never to let anyone get that close to him again. He sat there for a long time pondering his future and what he wanted out of life. Maybe he should just hook up with another team and keep doing what he knew how to do best. He was a good communications expert, hell; he was one of the best in the world. There wasn't any communication system that he couldn't operate he had proven that many times. On one mission to the orient, his had been destroyed by gunfire, and he had confiscated an Arabian radio system and rigged it so he could at least send Morse code to get help. Oh well, no big decision had to be made right now, he would just see how everything went. As the sun slowly went behind the evening clouds he closed his eyes and drifted off to sleep.

"What an arrogant son of a bitch!" Penny shouted as she opened the door to Julia's house. She had been removing dust covers, opening windows, and generally trying to get the musty smell out of the house. She tried to do this at least twice a month but she wasn't always as punctual as she should be. Penny stormed into the kitchen. "Got anything to drink?" she asked.

"Not unless you want some three week old lemonade or a glass of water. I have some peach brandy left over from the last party we had, but I wouldn't drink too much of it if I were you. What is wrong anyway? You and Jared already fighting?" Julia asked.

"I don't know if you could call it a fight or not but we had words and he got out of the car and told me that he might call and then again he might not." Penny replied.

"It all started with that damned Danielle speeding by us flirting and when he asked me about her I got the jealous bone out. One word led to another and he basically told me to back off and cool down some."

"And what did you do?" Julia asked.

"I left his ass walking down the dirt road to your cottage. He was limping a little, but maybe it will give him some time to cool off himself. Oh, to hell with him anyway, he isn't the only man in the world, I'll just find someone else to have around and he can kiss my ass!"

"Come out here on the porch and lets talk," Julia said. "You have seemed to be happier with him than I have seen you in a long time. What is it with you? Every time you find someone you like, you dig until you find something to run him off for. I think you are in love with your ex-husband, cannot have him, so you don't want to have anyone, is that the case? Because if it is, you are in for a terribly lonely life. Move on, Penny, he was a jerk, not to mention a womanizer, hell; he slept with Danielle your supposed best friend. I don't know that for sure, but she has told several people the same story. I don't know if it is supposed to make her feel better or not, but she is spreading it around. Jared seems like a nice guy, I am sure he has some faults, but there isn't anyone in the world that is perfect; male or female. If you like someone well enough to try to make things work with them, then you just have to work on the bad stuff. You may not be able to completely fix whatever the problems is, but you sure as hell can find a way to make it easier to cope with. Give it some time, that is, if you want to; if not then just run him off like you have done the rest of them in the last two or three years."

"Maybe you are right," Penny said. "I guess I expect too much from them, and maybe I just think they will all do me the same way. I hope he isn't still too mad at me. Where do you think he is?"

"My guess is that he has found the beer I have left in the fridge and is probably watching the sun go down in the hammock. If you hurry you an get there before dark, or before he falls in the water and drowns, then how do you think you would feel?" Julia said.

Penny didn't say anything. She got up from the stool and gave Julia a hug. She almost ran out to the car and sped off down the street. By the time she had gotten back to the cottage, there was no sign of him in the house. She wandered around the back and walked towards the hammock. There he lay, he had finished the beer, and the bottle had fallen from his hand. She bent over and gently kissed him on the cheek. He opened his eyes and looked up at her.

"I am sorry, Jared. I guess I am too jealous for my own good. We have both been through some of the same things, and I know I can be less jealous if you will just give me a chance. We haven't been seeing each other very long, but I like you and would like to see you some more."

"I am sorry, too." He said. "Guess I was just having flashbacks from some old ghosts. What do you say we start all over again and see where it goes? I can only stay a couple of days before I have to go back, and I damned sure don't want to fuss and fight the whole time I am here."

She took his hand and led him back towards the cottage.

"Hungry?" she asked.

"Well it is about supper time, think Julia would like to get some dinner?" he asked.

"Naw, I think she just wants to be left alone. That was the old family home, and there are a lot of memories there. She hadn't shown this much interest in it in a long time. I think the thought of having Tristan there with her has gotten her in the "nesting" mode. Besides, when I was there this afternoon, she had mentioned something about cooking there just to make sure the appliances still worked. The house hasn't been used since her parent's died. Her mother went first, and shortly after that, her father died also. It was after that when she started staying out at the cottage. She said it was easier to take care of than the big house, and that she didn't feel quite so lonely in the smaller place; plus she loved the sunsets from the dock and the ebb and flow of the tides. Everything is still pretty much the same. The house if full of antiques and all of them are in just a good condition as they were the day they were put into the house. Even the old car in the basement is just like new. Mr. Deveraux bought it for his wife, and she never got rid of it. He thought she would look good in the little sporty sedan, but she would rather ride with him in his truck whenever they went somewhere. They were inseparable. I think that is why he didn't live very long, he died just a short while after her."

"Any other relatives?" he asked.

"Only a younger brother," she said. "But he moved away shortly after college and the only times he has been back is to attend his parents funerals. Julia tried to get him to move back, but he vowed that if he ever left, he would never come back. He lives in Colorado somewhere, nowhere near water. Julia finally had the house appraised, sent him one half of what the house and land was worth, and doesn't hear from him much."

Strange" he said, "but you never know about people. They change sooner or later."

About that time they walked into the cottage. He walked into the kitchen to put the bottle in the trash and as he turned around he saw her standing in the doorway. She walked over to him and gave him a soft kiss on the cheek. He looked into her eyes and saw the burning desire she had. He put his arms around her, and kissed her passionately. They stood there for a long time holding, kissing, caressing, and exploring each other. He picked her up and took her into the guest bedroom. As he moved the covers off the bed, she unbuttoned her blouse. They kissed again and almost tore each other's clothes off. As he laid her on the bed, she smiled with anticipation. The same anticipation she had the first night in the apartment over the garage. He was a fine man, and she would try her best to let the jealous bone stay hidden. They made love for the better part of the evening. Sometime during the night just before she drifted off to sleep, she looked into his eyes and simply said she was sorry. He gave her a soft touch on the cheek, brushed her hair back, and told her not to worry. Things would be what they would be; they would just have to weather some storms if it were meant for them to be together.

Julia had called Mrs. Perkins as soon as Penny had left. They worked into the evening and got quite a bit of the rearranging done. Sally Perkins had lived next to the Deveraux's for as long as Julia could remember. She and her mother would spend long afternoons on the back porch talking, swapping recipes, and just generally keeping up on what the latest scuttlebutt was on Tybee Island. Her husband had been killed in the early days of the war, and she never remarried. She never had any children and just helped Julia's mom with the kids anytime she could.

As they sat on the back porch sipping fresh coffee, Julia was reminded of the days that her mom and Mrs. Perkins would sit out there for hours.

"Tell me, Julia, what is it that has brought you back home?" Sally asked. "I overheard you and Penny talking about some guy, are you girls in competition?"

"No mam," she replied. 'She is just up to the same old tricks. She doesn't want to have a man around full time and she cannot do without one either. I have to get on her case about once every month or six weeks. If I don't, she will wind up like Danielle Bellefonte and be chasing every pair of pants that shows up around here. They are the ones who are at each other's throats. I swear, every man that Penny shows up with, Danielle tries to score. I don't know what it is with those two. Besides, I have fallen in love with the most wonderful man in the world." Then she told Mrs. Perkins the whole story of she and Tristan. By the time she finished it was dark and she was very tired.

"So when will Mr. Wonderful be coming home?" Sally asked.

"I'm not sure, he has some physical therapy to go through. He was basically asleep for almost three weeks, and after that he has to go to somewhere in Virginia to talk to some high-ranking officials about something that happened and why it did. I think they are going to let him recuperate here, and then make the trip later." She didn't want to, and actually couldn't tell her any of the particulars of the mission. If she did, the next thing she would know would be that the whole island would know the story and that wasn't going to happen to them. They said their goodnights and as she closed the door and locked it, she thought of the lighthouse at the end of the island. She also thought of Tristan and wondered what his thoughts were of at this time. She would turn in and give him a call tomorrow and find out if there were any news of when he may be leaving the hospital. Besides she had a good three more days of cleaning, dusting, and making sure that everything was in good working order. All of the appliances were on again and seemed to be in good working order. She would cook breakfast the next morning. The bacon and eggs that she had gotten at the store needed to be used. As she walked down the stairs to the basement she uncovered her SUV. She put the key in the ignition and it started immediately. She turned it off and as she started up the steps she thought about the old Ford that her mother never drove, but still had covered in the basement. Maybe Tristan could get it started if he wanted to. It would be fun to drive. She wandered over to the corner of the basement and lifted the front of the cover. The running horse emblem in the front grill was still as shiny as ever. She replaced the cover and walked up the stairs. As she reached her old room at the top of the steps, she stood there for a few minutes before she actually went inside. This was the last room she wanted to clean because she wanted to make it special. The big walnut canopy bed and matching dresser was just a beautiful as ever. She would go to the fabric store tomorrow and pick out some new linens and covers. She walked back down the stairs and turned on the TV. She lay on the couch and even though she was tired, she wasn't sleepy. She thought about the story she had started. She spent the next thirty minutes looking for her laptop. She remembered unloading it, but couldn't remember where. She looked in her suitcase, and there it was. She plugged the power cord into the receptacle and as she sat at the table, the love affair between the confederate officer and the southern belle came to life again. She could envision them walking hand in hand through the streets of Savannah. Strolling down River Street past all of the traders and their wares. Her imagination went wild. For the next three hours it was constant pounding on the keys. Love was in the air. She could envision Tristan as the officer and she as the southern belle. His silver gray hair under the cover of the military hat and his sword by his side, ready at a moment's notice, to do battle if necessary. She could envision him on his trusty steed leading the soldiers into battle also. The sword in his right hand and the reins of his horse in the other, he was the picture of freedom. Sometime around two a.m. she couldn't stay awake any longer. She closed the laptop, and lay back down on the couch. As she pulled the old quilt over her, she remembered the times her mother covered her up and kissed her goodnight. Hopefully it wouldn't be long before she could kiss someone goodnight again. As she slowly drifted off to sleep, her thoughts were of someone two hours away. She smiled and fell asleep.

Chapter Six

The doctor made his usual rounds and as he made his way to Tristan's little part of the ICU he found the reading of his chart very interesting. The nurses had gotten him up and walking already this morning. They wanted him to get back into shape as soon as possible. The commander walked through the doors to the unit just as the resident was leaving.

"How are you feeling today?" he asked.

"Seems to be more tolerable every day; the headaches are becoming farther and farther apart, and the neurosurgeon says that the swelling in my brain is going down and that I may just accidentally get back to normal. I am glad you are here. I wanted to personally thank you for all you did for Julia. She is a wonderful person and I am very lucky to have her."

"You know she stayed here every night until you came to your senses don't you?" he asked.

"Yes, she told me that she couldn't leave me. It is funny; she was the last thing I was thinking of before the explosion, and the first thing I thought of when I woke up. Actually she was the first thing I smelled when I came to my senses. As I was falling into the water, I saw the missile. It was almost like someone had stopped time and everything was frozen. You always hear that when you are dying your whole life passes before you. Mine didn't, but the last seven days I spent with her did. Just as the explosion occurred I felt a warm feeling all over.

By the way, has anyone figured out who is responsible for what happened?" he asked.

"Not really," the commander replied. "No one has come forth and claimed responsibility, but I really don't look for anyone to do so anyway. They aren't interested in getting notoriety for killing some soldiers who are in a small part of the world where things like this don't exist. I am interested in finding out how they knew you guys were coming. I know you were flying too low for the radar to pick you up, plus the bird had the latest radar jamming devices known to man, so that couldn't be it. The investigators will be here tomorrow. Are you up to talking to them?" he asked.

"Sure," Tristan replied. "I'll give them the same story I gave you. I don't know of anything else to say. I would love to roll back the clock, or even wake up in a different world where all of the guys who have been with me for the last five years could be coming up the elevator with a six pack and a pizza but we both know that isn't going to happen. They can believe it or not, I don't care. My life has made a dramatic change for the better. And I plan on taking advantage of the change."

"My door is always open, if you need anything just let me know." The commander said. "Sorry to hear about your unit, but I firmly believe that everything happens for a reason."

They shook hands and as the commander was leaving there was a message being e-mailed to him from Langley. The investigators would be there in two days to go through the formal debriefing. Tristan was getting better by the day and would be released soon. He would be given choice of his next tour of duty. There would be a formal meeting at Langley soon, and hopefully the incident would be put to bed.

The next week proved to be unsettling for some, and a relief for others. Tristan was put into a private room and the investigators came and questioned him for about seven hours. As tiring as it was, he was sure glad to get it over with. Penny and Jared spent about three days together and he got a call and had to fly back sooner than expected. Penny had met Danielle at the grocery store, and had a few words with her about Jared. Seems that Danielle had caught him coming out of the local drive in market and made a pass at him.

She even went as far as to give him her telephone number. Penny found the number in Jared's pocket and asked him about it. He told her of the incident in the drive in market and Penny went off about it. She had been driving around town for two hours looking for her when she saw Danielle's car in the grocery store parking lot. It didn't take her but a few minutes to locate her in the store, and the war was on. You would have thought that she was going to beat her right there in the store. Most of the patrons heard all of the conversation but the most profound statement, "Let me tell you something you two bit whore, you stay away from me and anyone that is close to me, do you understand?" was the loudest comment that was made. The store manager had to ask the girls to take their discussion outside, as he didn't think his grocery store was the place for them to be arguing over some new flame. They argued in the parking lot for a few more minutes, and Danielle left in a big hurry. She and Penny had been involved in discussions about men before, but never anything this serious.

Julia found most of what she was looking for to make the house more to her liking, and talked to Tristan every day. Mrs. Perkins came over to the house each day just to see if Julia needed anything, and also to find out when the source of her happiness would be coming.

The day before Tristan was to be released, he received a letter from the "General." There wasn't much to it other than to thank him for his heroic deeds and for cooperating with the investigators. He also told him that he had been given an unlimited leave and when he felt like coming back to active duty to simply let him know. He was free to leave as soon as the doctors would release him. When the doctors came in that afternoon, that was just what he intended on asking them. They ran him through another set of tests and found that everything looked like it was going back to normal. The headaches were farther and farther apart, and the physical therapy had made him strong enough to go on extended walks in the courtyard every day. They told him that he could leave anytime he thought necessary. He called Julia that evening and they talked for a long while. She had been busy with the house, and had wanted to come back for a visit, but he told her to stay there and that he would be leaving soon. When he told her the good news he could almost see the smile on her face over the phone. He told her that as soon as he found out when the flight would arrive at the Savannah airport, he would let her know.

"What flight are you talking about?" she asked.

"I am one of the passengers on a helicopter that is bound for Savannah tomorrow. They are providing transportation for some dignitaries who are touring the port. Anyway, I should be there sometime in the afternoon." They talked for a little while longer, and he said, "I think I will hang up and go to sleep. If

I keep on talking, I may run out of things to say, and then we won't have anything to talk about."

"I doubt that," she replied. "You may have ran out of things to say, but I have been making a list, it will take you a long time to answer all of the questions I have for you." She said.

He simply laughed, told her he loved her and bade her a good night.

As she hung up the telephone she anticipated what it would be like to have him with her again. She refilled her coffee cup, grabbed the old quilt, and headed for her desk. She had more ideas for the confederate soldier and the southern belle, she might as well work on her book, there was no way she was going to be able to get to sleep anytime soon. Every time she thought of Tristan a warm feeling came over her.

Sometime around midnight someone rang her doorbell. She thought this as strange; no one knew that she was there, at least no one but the neighbors. As she opened the door, there stood Penny. She had obviously been crying for a long time and couldn't seem to control herself.

"What in the world is wrong with you?" Julia asked.

"Jared just called me and we had a long discussion on the phone. He basically told me that he didn't want to see me anymore because I was too jealous and not trusting enough of him. We had words before he left and most of them were my fault because I thought he was screwing Danielle. I have made a really big mistake." Penny said.

"What kind of mistake?" Julia asked.

"I argued with him over the telephone and basically accused him of fooling around with her, and he told me to lose the phone number and don't ever call him again, that he had no intention of ever calling me or seeing me again. That I had no right to accuse him of such a thing, and even if he did fool around with her, that he wasn't married or even engaged to me and that whatever he did was actually none of my business. I have really screwed up, he was a really nice guy." As the tears flowed down her cheek she said; "Now he probably will never speak to me again."

"Come in and I'll fix us a pot of coffee, looks like this may take a while." Julia offered.

They walked into the kitchen and Penny sat down at the breakfast bar. Julia filled the coffee pot with water and the usual ten cups of coffee grounds and got out the Kleenexes.

She had never seen Penny in this much of a state over anyone, much less a man. She had sworn more than once that she would never marry again, and that all men were good for was just one reason. As she sat out the creamer and sugar she turned on the television for the late news. Most of the crimes in Savannah were of a mild nature. There had been any major bad news in quite some time. There was some late breaking news about someone being found dead in an automobile in the back section of Bonaventure Cemetery but no names were mentioned as they were still trying to figure out how it happened. Julia and Penny talked till after 3 a.m. and Julia told her just to stay there for the rest of the night. She really had no need making the trek back to Savannah this late, and she could just sleep on the couch and leave the next morning; besides the state of mind she was in, she might start crying again and run off the road or have an accident some other way. She told her that she would be going to the airport to pick up Tristan and they would be coming back to Tybee for a while.

The warm morning rays of the sun were shining through the kitchen windows as Julia started a fresh pot of coffee. Penny was still asleep on the sofa. She walked out onto the porch and looked for the newspaper. As usual the paperboy had missed the driveway completely and it had landed in the flowerbed. Mrs. Perkins was looking for hers also, and spoke to Julia as she bent over to pick it up. As she stripped the plastic covering from the paper, she almost fell up the stairs; there on the front page of the Savannah times was Danielle Bellefonte's picture. She had been murdered in her car and her body was found in the back section of the Bonaventure Cemetery the night before. The details were sketchy, but apparently there had been some sort of scuffle and she had been stabbed more than once. There was no weapon found at the scene, but the area was still closed and the authorities were still searching.

"Wake up," she said as she shook Penny on the shoulder. "Look at this, someone has killed Danielle."

They both spent the next hour reading the newspaper article and talking about the incident. There were no witnesses, although there had been information given by the manager of the local grocery store about an argument between Danielle and an unidentified female about someone they were apparently both dating. The manager had asked them both to leave and didn't have any more information.

"That would be me," Penny said.

'What are you talking about?" Julia asked.

"I was the one arguing with her in the store. I went there to whip her ass and tell her to leave Jared alone. She had been flirting with him ever chance she got and I was tired of it. It had been her mission in life to make every guy I saw or dated ever since we had that blow up after my divorce, and I wanted to put it all to a stop. We took it out into the parking lot and about the time I started to scratch her eyes out, I realized that it was a mistake and that I shouldn't lower myself to that standard. I got into my car and drove away. That's all, I promise. I haven't seen or talked to her since. I don't disagree that that little slut didn't get what she deserved, but she didn't get it from me." Penny said.

"Are you going to the police?" Julia asked.

"I don't know, what do you think I should do? Penny replied.

"I wasn't the only person who didn't like her. Hell, half of the women in Savannah have talked about running her out of town on a rail or at least pooling their money together and sending her on a one way trip to Alaska or somewhere she couldn't get back from. Maybe I should, I have nothing to hide. I admit that I would have liked nothing better than to slap her across those collagen filled lips of hers, but I didn't ever think about killing her."

"I'll go with you, if you need me to," Julia said. "They will ask you a bunch of questions about where you were for the last couple of days, have you been in town?"

"Yes," Penny replied. "I have been at the store, and also had dinner at the riverboat restaurant last night, but just drove around most of the night."

"I think I would go down to the station and tell them your side of the story. If you go to them, they are more likely to believe your story than if they have to find you. Besides, you have nothing to hide, do you?" Julia asked.

"Now what kind of question is that?" she shot back at her.

"I may be hard to get along with, and may be a little wild sometimes, but I damned sure didn't kill anyone. I wouldn't risk the rest of my life in jail for that little piece of trash!!"

"I didn't mean anything," Julia said. "I was just asking questions. You aren't lily white in some instances either, you know. It hasn't been that long since you were asked about an affair with that lawyer in Mobile, has it?"

"I told you about that, I didn't know he was married. I really thought that he worked a lot as lawyers usually do, and anybody can make mistakes, or do you forget about that guy that had you over a barrel a couple of years ago?" She fired back.

"OK, let's not start old arguments all over again." Julia replied. "We have already hashed all of this out more than once, let's just take one day at a time and I'll help you as much as I can. If you need a character witness, I'll be there, just go to the police station and get it over with. They may already have some suspects. I can name at least a dozen women myself who secretly would have liked to see her dead."

Lt. Daniel Storey had been in charge of the Chatham County sheriff's department criminal investigation unit for more than five years. Previous to that he was sergeant over the patrol division and knew the streets of Savannah like the back of his hand. He had not lost contact with the people who "ran" the streets since his promotion and prided himself on being able to solve crimes faster than most. As he stood in the garage where the forensics experts were checking out the Mercedes Coupe that Danielle drove, he wondered why there had not been any fingerprints left anywhere on the car. There were only traces of blood from her body, and no visual altercation had been observed. The CSI team was scouring the vehicle with a fine toothcomb and had yet to come up with any clues. The only thing out of the ordinary was a small bag of a powdery substance that appeared to be cocaine. The results had not been confirmed, but the field test with the chemicals from the officer's car preliminarily confirmed that was what it was. She had been known among her peers to be very wild and also that she liked men. There had been some accusations that she had a lesbian side also, but no one would own up to being with her, or admit that they knew anything for sure. Penny had called her a "slut" on several occasions, only because she would always bring up the fact that she had slept with Penny's husband more than once while they were married. Never in public, only when the two were somewhat alone or somewhere in a large building together would she bring it up. They had been good friends up until that happened.

Lt. Storey told them to keep looking and let him know if they found anything. When he exited the elevator, he started down the hallway that led to his office. As he passed the secretary's desk, she advised him that there was someone there to see him. After being informed that it was in regards to the murder, he didn't mind staying a little longer in the office order to get some information. He had planned on riding the streets and checking with his contacts to find out if there had been any scuttlebutt put out, anything would help, at this point they had no suspects and there had not been any strange people in town lately, just the usual run of tourists. As he entered his office there sat Penny and Julia. They introduced themselves and after he asked what they wanted, Penny told him the story of the altercation in the grocery store. This was a major breaking point in the case. He had anticipated that he would have to spend at least a week just finding out who that mysterious woman was, not to mention trying to figure out if she really had anything to do with the actual murder. Penny gave him the whole story, from the beginning. It took a little more than an hour for her to get it all out. The whole time Julia was looking at her cell phone just to make sure Tristan had not been trying to get in touch with her. After taking her name and the information she provided, he asked Julia what her involvement was in the case. She merely told him that she was friend of Penny's and had talked her into coming down to the station and giving this information instead of just waiting for them to find her. Although it was all recorded on the store's video surveillance cameras, it would have taken some time to find out who she was and get her in for questioning. She also told him that Penny had come to her house crying and had stayed with her the rest of the night.

"Got any idea who might have wanted to kill her?" he asked Penny.

"I don't know of anyone in particular," she replied "but the general scuttlebutt around town is that she would screw just about anyone who would sleep with her, that is anyone who might have some money or a prominent position in this county. She had been married three times, two ended in death and the last in a very bitter divorce. Several women have talked about doing some pretty crazy things to her, but I really don't think that any of them would actually do it. Her ex husband moved away after giving her a pretty sizable settlement, and that is what she has been living off of for the last two or three years."

"Well, don't make any plans to leave on any extended vacations very soon. I am not considering you a suspect at this time, but I would like to talk to you again when I have longer visit with you. I have just received the search warrant for her condo and I need to get over there and check it out. Thank you for coming in." With that he stood and shook hands with the both of them. He asked that they spend a few minutes with the secretary and give a statement of what they knew about the whole situation and leave contact numbers where they could be reached.

"As they started out the door he asked Julia, " aren't you the local author, Julia Deveraux?"

"Yes I am," she replied. "Are you a fan?'

"No, but my wife is, she has read all of your books. I was wondering."

"Sure," she said. She knew what the next question would be. Most of them start out that way.

"Do you have a copy here?" she asked.

"No, but she left one in my car the other night. It would make her very happy if you would autograph it for her." He followed them down the hallway and to the elevator. Just as the doors opened, her phone rang. It was Tristan. She tried to answer it, but the interference from the metal inside wouldn't let her get a good signal.

"Dammit" she cursed. She had been waiting for that phone call all day and now when it came, she couldn't answer it. As he pressed the button for level one of the basement-parking garage, he said. "My car is in the garage downstairs. I can meet you ladies out front, or you can ride down with me and I will give you a lift outside to the parking area."

"That would be fine," Julia said.

He opened the door to the black sedan and as he did, Julia urged Penny to sit in the front. She positioned herself in the back seat on the passenger's side. As they started out of the garage, she found the book in the back seat with her. She opened it and simply signed it the same way she always signed the books for people she didn't know:

Thank you and good luck. I hope you enjoy the story.

Julia Deveraux

She noticed that the book didn't have the dust cover on it and that several pages in the book had been dog eared as if the person who had been reading it would only read short parts of it before they had to stop. She just imagined that he was actually the one who wanted the book autographed and was afraid to let her know that. *Must have been a testosterone thing, she thought.*

They exited into the parking lot and as he let them out at her car, the phone rang again. It was Tristan.

"I am at the airport on the National Guard side. Sorry, I didn't have time to call when we left. Had to do some last minute talking with the people who are here too. "

"Stay right where you are, I am about ten minutes away, and will be there soon." As she closed the phone tears of joy welled up in her eyes.

"Is everything OK?" Penny asked.

"Yes, it is; it is very much ok." She said.

She dropped Penny off at her car and headed towards the airport. The last thing he said before getting out of the car was simply "I'll talk to you later."

Julia just simply said, "Yea, but not too soon, OK?"

Penny smiled as she drove away. She knew how she felt. She had felt almost the same way when she saw Jared; too bad that wouldn't be happening again.

CHAPTER SEVEN

There he stood, on the sidewalk outside the private entrance to the National Guard hangars. The last place you could get to without security passes. He looked very handsome in his uniform. Funny, he looked different than he had the last time she had seen him in it. She pulled up, put the car in park and didn't even turn off the engine; she didn't even shut the door. He picked her up, gave her a big hug and a kiss, and held her for a long time. He had one single long stemmed red rose in his hand.

"This is for you, just happened to be thinking about you at the airport before we left, and thought you might like this. It isn't real, but that just means that it will last longer.

She took it from him, and gave him a big kiss. He picked up his duffle bag and threw it in the back of the SUV.

"I have a surprise for you," she said. "Ok, I cannot wait," he replied.

"What is it?"

"Now if I told you, it wouldn't be a surprise. Just sit back and enjoy the ride." She said.

As the pulled onto the parkway, she told him of the events of the last few days. He had asked if Penny and Jared were still seeing each other, and she simply said no. He didn't know that Jared had been called back to Virginia; he just thought that they had been busy and he hadn't called. She told him of the problems that they had with the jealously and the altercation with Danielle. She also told him that Danielle had been found dead in her car in the cemetery.

"What do you think?" Julia asked. "Not sure, do you think she did it? It doesn't sound very good for the home team. Sounds like she had a motive, but according to what I remember you saying about Danielle before I left, there are probably several women in town who may have had the same motive. Jealously is a bad thing. I can see why Jared cut ties with her. His last girlfriend gave him a fit. He lived through hell; she was always checking his cell phone, asking him whom he had been talking to that day, and not giving him any leeway at all. That drives more men away than anything. I am sure if that was the case with Penny, he saw the same thing coming back and decided that it just wasn't worth it. Some men put up with it for a while, but if it gets too annoying then they just let it go. It is a matter of trust. If she trusted him, then she wouldn't be so damned nosy."

They passed the usual turn off to the cottage and he didn't really say too much. He just thought maybe they were running an errand of something. They turned on Forsythe drive and as they pulled into the driveway at the end of the street, he asked,

"Are we visiting someone here?" "No," she replied, "This is the surprise. This is my family's old home place. My parents left it to my brother and myself when they died. After a while he didn't want to have any part of it, so I just simply had the place appraised, bought out his half interest in it, and kept it. I stayed in the cottage because it was so much easier for one person to live there. I love this old place. I have spent these last few weeks cleaning and fixing it up for you. It has a beautiful garden in the back, it is with in walking distance to most of the places we like here on Tybee Island, and I thought that you might just like it better than the cottage. We can still go out there whenever you want, I just really like this place for us."

He walked up the front steps and onto the big wraparound porch. The architecture of the home was brilliant. It had all of the old wooden moldings and trellises of the period and they had been very well preserved. As he made his way around to the side, there sat the hammock. He simply turned and smiled at her, "is this the same one?"

"Yes, it is. I thought you might like it here. If you want to, we can get another one for the cottage, I just thought this would be a good place for this one. You can catch the same evening sunshine and listen to the waves from the ocean. We are only a block from the beach, and any given evening you can lie out here and hear the surf as it hits the beach. We can walk along the beach, and then come back to the house. I know how you liked the back porch at the cottage; I had hoped that you might like this just as well."

"It is wonderful," he replied. "Just like you. I love you, Julia. I have thought about you so much. I cannot begin to thank you for all you have done for me while I was in the coma. The doctors said that the exercises you gave me helped me recover my muscle strength back sooner than most people would have. They also said that your reading to me, talking to me, and everything else that you did, just hastened my recovery. I cannot ever repay you for that. He pulled her close and gave her a long kiss."

"I love you too," she said. "I just couldn't bear to think of you lying there not moving, I just knew that it would be only a matter of time before you would wake up. I prayed every night, every day, and sometimes all day. I knew God had brought us together; He was just trying to find out how bad we wanted to stay together."

They walked into the house and she gave him the tour. As they walked up the stairway to the second floor, he was amazed at the furnishings. She opened the door to her bedroom, and said. "This is where I would like for us to sleep, if you have no objections."

She took his hand and led him over to a set of French doors that led out onto a balcony. It was big enough for two chairs and a small table. The soft rays of the evening sun were sneaking through the Spanish moss on the trees, and as the sun set lower in the west, they stood there for a long time.

"My staying here with you isn't going to sully your reputation, is it?" he asked.

"Not in the least." She replied. " I really don't care who knows, it isn't any of anyone's business but ours. We can stay here for as long as we want. Mrs. Perkins is the neighbor next door, and she is really the only one on the block who is sociable enough to come over anyway. I will warn you, though, she will talk your ear off; but she is a wonderful cook. She makes the best sweet potato pie in the south."

" I cannot wait," he replied with a smile.

They went back downstairs and she took him to the basement. She showed him where the old Chevy was. He asked if the SUV was a recent purchase, and she said no. She said that she had bought it several months ago with some of the money her parents had left her. She said that she hadn't driven it much and left it in the basement. He inquired about the vehicle in the other corner of the basement and she told him the story of the car and how her mother liked it, but didn't drive it very much. He lifted the cover off it and asked how long it had been since it had run.

"I think it was started last year. I used to come down here once a week and start it, then it got to once a month, and then it got to a couple of months, and then I just quit. Mr. Perkins filled the crankcase with oil and said if I wasn't going to drive it that would keep the engine from "seizing up" as he put it. "There aren't too many of these left." He said. "Most of them are in museums or in some old rich codger's garage and it is only driven on Sundays."

"Well, if you would like to fool with it, then maybe we can get it running, and drive it some on Sundays ourselves." She said.

"Ok, it is a deal. Just make sure it gets on my honey do list that I know you have already started for me."

They both laughed and started back up the stairs. It was getting late in the evening and he had plans for them tonight; probably some of the same plans that she also had.

Tristan and Julia made their way into the kitchen and started preparing dinner.

"Why don't you just sit there and let me do this? You are the one who needs the recuperation." She said.

"Not a bad idea, I guess, I am just not used to someone taking care of me." He said.

"Well, you can get used to it, I'll do as much as you will let me. I am the doctor here on Forsyth Drive, and you are the patient."

He smiled and gave her a soft pat on the rear. She directed him to the refrigerator and told him that he needed to pick out a bottle of wine for dinner. She had been to the liquor store last week and brought some home for experimentations.

"There is a space for a wine cellar in the basement." She told him. "Maybe we can start collecting some for it."

Across town Penny Oglethorpe was closing up her antique shop. She had two choices for dinner; frozen entrees, or a stop at one of her favorite spots. Lt. Daniel Storey stopped by the local cigar store. His wife wouldn't like it any, but he was ready for a good Macanudo. The CSI team was still searching Danielle's apartment. They turned up nothing in the car. If there had been any prints, someone had wiped them clean or worn gloves. The preliminary report from the apartment was that nothing was out of place. The apartment was as clean and neat as her car had been. Not even any dirty dishes in the sink. There were some leftovers in a carryout box in the fridge, but nothing to say where they were from. Dan told them to keep searching and to call and let him know if anything was found. He hadn't much more than gotten home until he got the call.

"You probably should come over here, we found a diary hidden between the mattresses and it has some pretty juicy stuff in it. We started to read it to find out whether or not it may have any bearing on the case. There are names, dates, meeting places, an some other stuff." He said.

"OK, I'll be there in about ten minutes."

He kissed his wife goodbye and told her that he may be a while. She knew this whole thing had him pretty upset. There hadn't been anything like this happen in a long time.

"I'll keep dinner warm for you." She said. He just smiled, gave her a hug and a kiss, and closed the door behind him.

Danielle Bellefonte's apartment was located in the upper middle class part of town. There was a gated entrance, and security guards twenty-four hours a day. It had almost taken an act of congress to get access to her place. They had to get a search warrant issued and delivered to the manager before he would let them in. Even though it was a murder investigation, he was afraid that the bad publicity would cause some of the tenants some unrest. None of the neighbors had seen her in a few days. The last time she was seen, she was leaving with a gentleman who followed her out of the parking lot. She was in her Mercedes and the young man who had visited her was driving a black Lexus. No one had gotten a license number or had much of a description. Dan walked up the stairs to the second floor and as he walked in the front door he was somewhat taken aback with the furnishings. Everything in the room seemed to be some sort of Indian antiques. The statues and small figurines of elephants, monkeys, and other animals dominated the tables and bookshelves. As he entered the bedroom, which was the largest room in the unit, it had the motif of an Egyptian king. The colors and accents were perfectly matched.

"Boy, she had some taste, didn't she?" he commented to the sergeant.

"Yea, and not only in furniture either." He said.

As he opened the drawer, there were several different types of female articles of pleasure. He handed the diary to Dan and as he read the last couple of entries he thought of Penny.

Apparently Danielle had run into Jared at one of the local drive in markets and asked him if he would like to go for a ride. He declined and said that he wasn't interested in her. She had told him that if he tried being with her just once, he wouldn't want to go back to that hateful jealous bitch he was fooling around with. Apparently Jared had told her that he had to leave town for a while, and that he wouldn't be coming back any time soon. Danielle told him that was ok; she gave him her telephone number and simply said that if he wanted to be with a real woman, he could call her. She would even meet him somewhere outside of town if need be.

"I am going to take this with me, make a note in the report that it was found and it was turned over to me. Have you read any of the other entries?" he asked.

The sergeant simply replied, "No sir, we figured that it might have some pretty interesting information about some other folks in this town, and we felt it would be better off in your hands instead of ours."

"Good idea," he replied. "Now if you don't need me for anything else, I will go back home and enjoy my dinner."

With that he walked back down the stairs. The investigation of the apartment was almost finished anyway, and it would be sealed until further notice. As he drove back to his house, he picked up the diary. Wonder what, or better still who is in here? She must have led some sort of crazy life. I guess I'll have to read into this to try and find out if there are any suspects who may have been involved in this.

As he pulled into the driveway, he noticed that the interior lights were on inside the house. He opened the trunk and laid the diary inside. That probably would be the safest place to have it; he didn't want his wife looking into it while he was asleep. Besides, it was part of the investigation and he didn't need it at home anyway. He would stop at the local coffee shop in the morning and look into the book while he was having his first cup.

Besides the diary had already been dusted for fingerprints and apparently there were none other than the owner's on it. As he walked up the sidewalk to the front door, he thought that is was awful strange that nothing was adding up. Oh well, maybe things would change tomorrow morning. As he opened the door his wife, Margie, met him.

"I know you have had a hard day, come into the kitchen. I have warmed up your dinner, and we can talk."

Chapter Eight

Penny kicked off her shoes and shut the door as she entered the living room. She sat the Chinese food down on the coffee table and turned on the television. Retiring to the bedroom to change clothes, she opened the newspaper and laid it on the bed. There on the front page was the story of Danielle's untimely death. There weren't any gruesome photos, but the narration the reporter had given left little to the imagination. She had been found dead in her car, stabbed three times in the chest. There had been no evidence of any type of struggle and the murder weapon had not been recovered; nor had any clues either. She walked back into the living room and sat down at the coffee table to try and enjoy her meal in peace. The local news wasn't very far from airing, and she wondered if it would be on there also. She turned the television off and tried to put it all out of her mind. The light on the answering machine was blinking and upon examination she found that she had three messages waiting. She sat the plate on the table and pushed the button. As she was almost back to the sofa the messages came on. The first two were just annoying solicitors, but the last one was from Jared. He told her that he was sorry that he had been so mad and that he would be calling her in a couple of weeks to see if maybe they could talk some more. He had been given a temporary assignment and it would be a while before he could call her again. Her heart raced. She didn't know what to say. She figured she would never hear from him again. But what kind of assignment would he be on? Would it be dangerous like the one that Tristan just finished? This was crazy. She wanted to call Julia and talk to her, but she knew better. She would talk to her tomorrow and maybe get some inside info from Tristan as to where Jared may be and what he might be doing.

Tristan and Julia finished dinner and a bottle and a half of wine. They sat on the porch after cleaning the kitchen and for a few minutes were silent. He knew what was coming next so he just thought he would get it out in the open.

"I have two weeks before I need to go to Virginia." He started. "I have a meeting with some people who are going to try to talk me into staying in the service. I admit that I like the adventure and seeing the different places in the world, but I think that part of my life is over for me. I have never met anyone like you and I would like to spend some time getting to know you better. Do you realize that I don't know what your favorite color is, what your favorite season of the year is, or even if you like children? We had a whirlwind romance and a lot of things have happened in the last few weeks. I have lost some of the best friends that I have ever had. Not only have we faced danger together numerous times, but also we have had some of the best times together that I have ever experienced. But one thing I know now that I never thought about before was it could all change in an instant. Meeting and falling in love with you has changed my whole out look on life."

He put his arm around her and gave her a gentle kiss on the forehead.

"You aren't going to get off that easy," she said. And sat her glass on the table beside the swing. She turned and gave him a long passionate kiss. She turned and maneuvered herself into his lap. As they sat there holding each other in the moonlight, they kissed and hugged each other for a long time.

"I never knew it could be like this," she said. "I write these things in my books every time, and never really thought that something this good could be happening to me. You see other people who are apparently happy in their relationships, but sometimes it just seems out of reach for some of us. I love you too, Tristan. I never believed in love at first sight, but no one has ever made me feel quite like you have. I feel like I have known you all of my life." She replied.

He stood up with her in his arms and she grabbed the door handle. He carried her over the threshold and closed the door with his foot. As he started up the stairs, she asked,

"Are you sure you are up to this?"

"If I can make it up the stairs without having a heart attack, then we will be just fine."

They both laughed.

He took her into the bedroom and laid her across the canopy bed. She had lighted some candles after dinner in anticipation of being there soon. She slowly undressed and as he walked towards the bathroom to take a shower he turned around. She had followed him across the room, removing her clothes as she walked. She playfully slapped him on the butt as he entered the shower.

"Mind if I join you?" she asked.

"I would be terribly disappointed if you didn't." he said.

They stood in the shower for a long time. Reminiscing about the first time they made love, the first shower they had taken together, and the feelings they had for each other. They slowly soaped and massaged each other's bodies until they couldn't stand it any longer. The passion in the shower rose higher and higher. Eventually they had to turn off the water for it ran cold. They dried each other off and found themselves lying beside each other on the crisp clean sheets. She created her favorite place nestled against his chest with his arms wrapped around her.

"Remember the last time we were here?" she asked.

"Yes, I do," he replied. "But I am not leaving you tomorrow. I won't leave you for any longer than I have to. Will you marry me?"

WOW! This came unexpectedly. She had relished the thought of becoming Mrs. Tristan Broward, but she had no idea that he would ask her this soon.

"Are you sure that is what you want?" she asked.

"I know we haven't known each other very long, Julia. But I cannot bear the thought of leaving you. You know I have to go to Virginia for a meeting soon, and when I do, I am going to request my retirement. I have given the best days of my life to my career and now I want to spend the best of the rest of my days with you. It doesn't have to happen tomorrow, just think about it and we can discuss it later. I have money invested in some mutual funds and have made some other sound investments over the years, not to mention my military pension. If you never did anything else we could live comfortably." He said as he gently ran his fingers through her hair.

"I am not worried about finances, Tristan." She replied.

"My parents left my brother and I their life savings and plus what I have made on the royalties from my books along with the investments I have made, we could live very comfortably. I just want to make sure that is what you want. I would like nothing better, but let's just take it one step at a time. The answer is yes, if that is what you want to know right now, but we can continue to carry on with our lives. If you are afraid of what people would say about us living here together, don't, I have never lived my life based on what other people think, and I am not going to start now. I love you also, and want to spend the rest of my life with you." She said.

He kissed her softly on the back of her neck and gently caressed her closer to him. As the moonlight passed gently through the curtains, they tried to make up for lost times. It was like the last night they had spent together, except this time he would not be leaving in the morning. Tomorrow was another day, another adventure, and the start of a new life together.

Julia awakened to the aroma of fresh brewed coffee. She hadn't noticed that Tristan had gotten up and went downstairs. He appeared in the bedroom with a tray. Scrambled eggs, bacon cooked just to her liking, and French toast. She sat up in the bed just as he sat the table across her lap. Never before had anyone been thoughtful enough to bring her breakfast in bed.

"I could get used to this," she said. "This is a first for me."

"I cannot believe that, I would think that someone would love to have the opportunity to see you naked in the morning and eat breakfast with you. When you awake in the morning, you steal the rays from the sunshine."

With that he sat down on the side of the bed. "Where's yours?" she asked.

"I've already eaten, had my morning walk, and actually was afraid that you might be awake before now." He answered. "You were sleeping so good, I didn't want to wake you, thought you might need the rest after last night." He said with that silly little grin that he always gives her with the wink.

"I wasn't the one who went to sleep first," she playfully replied. "I think I remember someone snoring lightly as they finally laid their head down on the pillow."

He took another sip of his coffee and simply replied, "I don't understand the question."

They talked for a little while longer as she savored the food. She didn't realize just how hungry she was. After she finished her breakfast, he removed the tray and she headed towards the bathroom. As she got to the door, she turned around and smiled. He had remembered that smile from the first night they had spent together in the cottage.

"Not this morning," he said with a grin. She tried to form a little pout, but finally had to laugh. He walked down the steps to the kitchen and as he put the dishes in the sink, he heard a knock at the door.

"Who could it be at this time of the morning?" As he opened the door, there stood Penny Oglethorpe. He invited her in and offered her a cup of coffee. As she sat at the breakfast bar he sat the cup in front of her.

"Is Julia home?" she asked.

"Yes, she is upstairs in the shower." He replied.

"She should be down shortly. Can I get you anything else?"

"No," she replied.

She sat there speechless for a long time. Shortly Julia came down the stairs. By this time Tristan had walked out onto the porch to give them some privacy. He sensed that she wanted to talk to her alone.

"What are you doing here so early?" she asked.

"You never get up before nine and what are you doing out here?"

"I have to talk to you about Danielle."

"What is there to talk about?" Julia asked.

"She kept a diary. It has information on all of the people she had fooled around with.

Names, dates and times, where they went and even what she did to some of them. I didn't know about it until we got into the argument a few days before she was found dead. As you know we were best of friends until something happened. Then she turned on me like a viper."

"What happened that could be so bad, and what are you afraid of?" Julia asked.

"We went to this party one night. One of those toy parties where only women go. We had a few glasses of wine, looked at some of the adult samples and even purchased some. I figured that if I wasn't going to have a man with me most of the time, I should have a substitute. Anyway we came back to my place and drank a little more. Some time later I just told her to sleep here on my sofa because I was afraid for her to drive. Shortly after I got to sleep she came into the bedroom and came on to me...."

"She did what?" Julia said with a loud gasp.

"She came on to me, she said that she had wanted to sleep with me for a long time, but was always afraid to tell me."

"What did you do?" Julia asked.

"What do you think I did? You don't think I actually would do something like that, do you?"

"No, I don't, but I never could believe that as close as you two were, that you could be so mad at each other." Julia said.

"You don't know her, Julia. She was crazy. She would wake up in the middle of the night and just leave, and not come back for two or three days. You know how last year she left for a week and no one knew where she was. And another thing, my antique silver letter opener is missing. I looked for it yesterday to open some mail, and it was gone. I have a bad feeling about this. What do you think I should do? Should I go to the authorities and tell them truth or just wait until they read the diary and come to me?"

"Do you think she wrote that down?" Julia asked.

"I don't know, she got mad at me and told me that she wrote everything in that book and that if anyone ever asked she would tell them that I was one of the best lovers she ever had. How sick can that be?" Penny asked.

"Why are you worried about the letter opener?" Julia asked.

"I just have an uneasy feeling about this whole thing. I am going to the authorities and see if there was anything said. I'll call you later."

With that she walked out the door, got into her car, and left. Julia stood there for a long time trying to put the whole story together. Danielle was wild and crazy at times, and there was speculation that she was having affairs with a couple of prominent people, but who would have thought that someone would just murder her and leave her body in the cemetery?

Dan sat down at the window table in the coffee shop and took off his coat. It was about 6:30 a.m. and the regular morning crowd wouldn't be there for another hour or two. Margie was still asleep when he had left and he didn't have the heart to wake her up. As he opened the diary, the only thing on the first page was her name written in female cursive simply *Danielle Bellefonte.* No address, no phone number, nothing, just her name. As he started reading he realized that the first entries were almost three years old. As he thumbed through the pages it seemed to drift from one place to the other. There were entries from vacations, business trips with her ex husband, things they had done, thought about doing, and dates and times of the places they had visited. As he got further into the book, the divorce had already happened and she was seeing a couple of prominent people in town. The only problem was that one of them was married at the time they were seeing each other and to Dan's knowledge they were still together. There were notes, dates, and times when Danielle would make phone calls to him and demand money. It started out in small sums, but there were entries towards the end of the records that involved five figures. The red Mercedes coupe she drove was registered to a rental agency in Mobile. Dan had already checked it out. It was rented in her name for two years and the fee was paid for in cash; up front. There were a few blank pages and then all of a sudden was an entry of a party. The names of some of the participants were listed, but the main one that was underlined twice was that of Penny Oglethorpe. She had told the story that she and Penny went to this party, got pretty high on the wine, and after a few more at Penny's apartment, they slept together. Danielle said that Penny had resisted at first, but succumbed to the wine and the consistent longing by Danielle. She had said that she loved Penny for a long time, but not like this. They had never done this before, and she couldn't get her to do it again. Drunk or sober. The last three written pages mentioned a young man whom she had just met. No name was mentioned and nothing much more than a few graphic details about how they had just met in a bar, and when they went outside to get into their vehicles they talked and made out for a long time. He offered for them to have the thrill of sex in the backseat of his Lexus in the parking lot and she was game. She made the comment that it was the most exciting thing she had ever done. She had called him the next day to try to set up another meeting and he told her that it was just a one-night stand and that he could never see her again. He was married and he was sorry that he had taken the chance with her. He regretted it.

This made her very mad as no one had ever turned her down before. She told him that he had to meet her or she would tell his wife everything. At this point Dan had pretty much sized up the motive. She was blackmailing someone, but whom? Why would she want to meet in Bonaventure, and how did the guy wipe the car so clean?

Across the street from the coffee shop he sat. He had recognized the book that Dan was reading. She had told him about it and even showed it to him once when he had visited her at noon. He knew that it was a bad choice, but he couldn't help himself. It was if she had cast a spell on him and he couldn't get her off his mind. He had followed her to the bar and even watched as she and the guy made love in the back seat of the car. That was what had made him angry, she had turned him down for the night, yet she was there acting like a whore. What has come over me, I have never had a woman do this to me before. I wonder what he is going to do with the diary? I cannot show my hand and ask him, if I am mentioned in those pages then he will be asking me some intimate questions. I guess if I am mentioned then he will contact me soon enough. I wish I had never spent the night with her. No one but my ex-wife knows of my fantasies and I regret actually acting them out, especially with Danielle. Playing games with your wife is one thing, playing them out with another woman is something else. With this he looked at his watch; it was time for him to get to the office, he couldn't be late. He had to figure out a way to dispose of the letter opener. He had taken it from Penny's desk at the antique shop just two weeks before. He couldn't justify buying it, but he just had to have it. He had never seen anything like it before, and he knew that if it were discovered at his apartment, it would be a lot more to explain than a knife or some other weapon. He had to stop Danielle from the things she was doing, even if it meant killing her. He had planned to give her the letter opener as a present, but when he offered it to her, she laughed at him. He knew of her other friends, but he didn't have the money that they did. He couldn't give her those expensive gifts, but he could give her his love. But she didn't want that. He had suggested they meet at the cemetery maybe she would "play games " with him in her car. But when he started kissing her, she pushed him away. He couldn't stand it any longer. Before he knew it he took the letter opener and stabbed her with it. He didn't remember how many times, he just did it. He took the cloth he had it wrapped in and wiped the door, the window, and the seats as best as he could. He then shut the door and ran through the "Garden" and finally made it to his automobile parked on the backside of the property. There had been no one else in the cemetery at that time. This part of it had been a favorite parking place of thrill seekers who had fetishes about ghosts. He would dispose of the letter opener later. He had to get home.

Watching Dan with the book brought back too many memories. The flashbacks of her gasping for breath, and the look on her face were something he couldn't forget. The look on her face was still as fresh as it was the night of the murder. He would never forget it, not as long as he lived. He got up from the table, got into his car and headed towards the office.

❧

Dan jotted down some notes and made a preliminary list of some people he had to talk to. As he drove to the office, he wondered just what these people's reactions were going to be. Two of these guys could be really hurt business wise and personally if this information got into the wrong hands; not to mention what would happen if the information Danielle wrote about the woman who visited her last. One thing was certain, he couldn't let anyone else see this, not even the district attorney, at least until he had gotten some advice from a long time friend.

As he walked into the judge's office the smell of the cigar was prominent.

"You know you aren't supposed to smoke in municipal buildings don't you your honor?" Dan said with a laugh.

"What are you going to do lieutenant, put me in smoker's jail?" The judge replied.

"Grab one and lets go out on the balcony, that way they cannot say anything about it, what are you here for, got another parking ticket you need fixed?"

Judge Robinson was a general sessions judge. He heard minor complaints, traffic dockets, and misdemeanor cases. He and Dan had been friends for a long time. They met when Dan was a patrolman and he had just opened his law practice. His parents had owned the local printing business, but he just couldn't stomach the idea of working behind a press all of his life like his father had. He and Dan had given each other advice over the years, but this was different, he needed the judge's advice on how to continue with the information he had. He was one step from calling in the federal authorities before he came up with the idea that he needed some judicial advice. Dan pulled up the old patio chair and reached into his coat pocket for his snip. It was always good to come and talk to the judge; he always had a good cigar in the humidor on his desk. The doctor had told him years ago that he shouldn't be doing this, but he wouldn't listen. The third floor balcony of the Chatham county courthouse was a good place to enjoy conversation and a fine cigar. The early morning sun was still behind the trees and according to the weatherman; the cool air would be with them for a while. The judge had been in this office for the better part of twelve years. Twice a day he would sit on the balcony overlooking the streets below. Once in the morning and once in the afternoon. He had adjourned court many a day just to come and sit outside. Of course, the lawyers had objected to him just up and continuing a case, but there hadn't been a one of them that hadn't come for his advice at one time or another. Dan snipped the end of the cigar and as he was pulling the "torch" out of his vest pocket, the judge asked,

"You're here about the girl, aren't you?"

"How did you know?" Dan asked.

"Well, from the stories in the newspapers, the knowledge that you had her diary and wouldn't let anyone else look at it, and the fact that most of the time you come here when you have something that you cannot handle alone, I'd say that was right, huh?" The judge said.

"Yes, you summed it up pretty good. It is a big piece of evidence in the case, but there are some pretty incriminating things in there, and I thought I would ask you if you thought we just might need to bring someone in on the federal level because of the implications." Dan replied.

"Anybody we know?" he asked.

"I am afraid so, even someone who would be potentially involved in the proceedings." "That is not good," the judge said. "Do you want to tell me or are you going to make me read the damned thing?"

"I think you should read it your self, and that way, I couldn't be accused of leaking information. The press has been calling me all morning, since about 5 a.m. and I am not ready to talk to them just yet. I will have to talk to the district attorney later today, but he isn't going to like what I tell him."

"Is he mentioned in the book?" the judge asked.

"I'll let you read it, he is one of the players. Their professions identify most of the ones implicated. The most important ones are just mentioned as the attorney, the policeman, or the doctor. We know two doctors who practice in town, two attorneys whom have been seen with her in public, and I haven't a clue who the policeman is supposed to be. That might just be the one we are looking for. He would know just how to cover up the evidence and how to not leave any fingerprints or clues at the crime scene."

"Has the D A asked for the evidence yet?" the judge asked.

"No, but I haven't talked to him yet this morning either. I have sent both of his calls to voice mail, and have purposely not gone to my office yet for fear of running in to him. I think I will stay out a little while longer; maybe go back to the scene and see if there maybe, just maybe, is something the forensic guys missed. I know they are pretty thorough. But sometimes they make mistakes just like we do. Anyway, take a look at it, and let me know what you think. I'll be back after lunch and we can talk about it."

Dan crushed out the remainder of the cigar and walked out of the office.

Damned shame, the judge thought. She was such a pretty girl, and lots of fun to be around too.

Just as Dan was walking through the security gates at the front of the courthouse, the Assistant District Attorney came through the front door. As the passed in the hallway, he asked,

'I understand that you had some evidence that needs to be checked in."

"Could be, could not; I haven't decided yet. When I decide, you will be the first one I tell, that is unless the general is in, then I will hand deliver it to him personally."

"You cannot withhold evidence, Dan, you know that. It has to be accessible to the prosecution in a felony case." He said with a louder than usual voice.

"You will get your damned chance to see it, when the time comes. Right now the secrecy of the information is of the utmost importance in this case. If it gets out, some of the prime suspects just may get the idea to leave town. I'll let you know when you can have it." Dan replied.

"Right now, I have some witnesses to interview."

He walked across the street and turned on the block to the antique store. As he reached for the handle, he noticed that it was still locked from the night before. He left one of his business cards in the mail slot and turned and walked away. He thought for a minute, and turned and walked back to the door. Something was strangely missing. Penny always puts out the open/closed sign. He tried the door again and it was still locked. But there was no sign in the door. He made a mental note of the surroundings and walked back to his car. By the time he got back to the vehicle his cell phone was ringing again. This was the fourth time the district attorney general had called. He flipped open the receiver and simply said hello. There was no one on the other end. About the time he was about to hang-up, the voice said. Please come up to my office; I need to talk to you, alone. With that the connection was lost. Dan stood there silent for a moment. Should he go to the judge's office and get the book, or should he just go up there cold and find out what he wanted. Oh to hell with it, he started toward the front steps and into the lobby. He made his way to the elevator and as he stepped inside, he pushed the button for the second floor. When the doors slid open, there he stood, with the strangest look on his face. Alexander Graham, the meanest district attorney in the state of Georgia; or at least that was what the governor said about him. They met at a fundraiser a few years back and never liked each other since. The governor never missed a chance to poke him in the ribs about something and neither did he. Alexander stretched out his hand and Dan took it reluctantly.

"What can I do for you, General?" he asked.

"Kindly step into my office, if you don't mind. I would like to talk to you about a private matter." They entered the office through Alexander's entrance that led straight into his private office. He didn't waste any time.

"I understand that you have a publication that might just be important to the Bellefonte murder investigation. If that is the case, then I need for you to turn it over for informational purposes. We have some other evidence that we need to compare to the publication." He said.

"Bullshit," Dan said.

"You don't have squat. They are still processing the car, the apartment, and anything else she has touched in the last two months. The book stays with me, there is some incriminating evidence in there, and I am not giving it to you or anyone else outside of the federal marshal's office."

""Then when do you think we may get the chance to examine it?"

"I don't know, but when I do, you will be the first one to see it, until then, don't ask me anymore."

He turned around, let himself out the same door, and walked down the hall. He passed up the elevator, and went for the stairs. Trying to collect his thoughts, he didn't pay any attention to the man who passed him in the hallway. He bolted down the stairs and out the exit. He would go back to the cemetery, just to take a look around himself.

Julia loaded the groceries in the back of her vehicle. She had left Tristan at home working on his computer, getting ready for his trip to Virginia. As she drove past the antique shop she noticed that the open sign had not been put up. She looked at her watch and thought this was strange. Penny was always there by this time. She picked up her cell phone and tried to call her. No answer, it went directly to voice mail. On the way out of town back to Tybee Island she purposely drove by Penny's place. No vehicle there either. She would go back home, put up the groceries and try again.

Jared poured another glass of wine and sat down on the side of the bed. He had returned to Savannah and called Penny. He told her that he didn't want anyone to know he was in town, as he didn't know how long he had to stay. It seemed funny to her, but with everything that had happened she wasn't one to make comments about strange stuff. They had spent the night together, talked and slept most of the day, and were enjoying the take out from the Mexican restaurant.

"Thanks for coming," he said. "I really don't have much time, the doctors have released me and I have to leave in two days. I don't know how long I will be gone, but I wanted to see you before I left."

"Have you heard about Danielle?" She asked.

"Yes, I read it in the paper when I was waiting for you. The newspaper must have been old. Do they have any suspects?" he asked.

"Don't know, they haven't gotten around to me yet, but I am sure that I will get the call pretty soon." At that point she told him the story of the party night and all of the events that led up to and beyond the incident at her apartment.

"I never figured you for a lesbian, Penny. You like natural sex too much." He said.

"I don't know if I should take that for a compliment or an insult, but I'll take it as a compliment." She said. They talked for a few more minutes and she asked him what she should do.

"If you know they are going to question you, it would be better for you to go to them instead of waiting for them to come to you."

"Ok, then I will call the police department tomorrow and go in and tell them what I know." she said.

"I have a flight to catch tonight from Jacksonville. I'll call you as soon as I can if you would like. I'm not making any promises Penny, but I would like to see you again. I am not asking you to be exclusive with me, as you well know, in this business; I may not ever show up again. Just follow your heart." He said.

A short while later she was in her car and on the way back to her house. She liked him very much, but she just had the gut feeling that she would never see him again. As she drove by the shop, she noticed something sticking in her door. She stopped and retrieved the business card that Dan had stuck in the door. She reached for her cell phone, and had forgotten to turn it back on. There were three unheard messages; two of them were from Julia. She called her number and for the next twenty or so minutes gave her the four one one on what had been happening for the last 24 hours. She told Julia about finding the card and said that she was going to the authorities because she was tired of the waiting game. Julia told her that she thought that was the best idea. If she went in on her own, they would be less likely to suspect her. Just as she hung up the telephone, Tristan walked into the kitchen. "I have finished with what I needed to do, want to get out of here for a while?" He asked.

"No, darling, I have some things I need to do and must get them done today. Why don't you take a walk or go down to the beach for a while?" She said.

With that he kissed her on the cheek and told her that he would go exploring. He hadn't been walking in a couple of days and needed the exercise. He told her that he had to be in Virginia in three days and had already made arrangements for the flight. There were more visitors coming to Savannah so he could hitch a ride back to Jacksonville with them, and then take a military plane to Virginia. She blew him a kiss as he walked out the door. She finished putting up the groceries and went to her desk to make some phone calls. Her agent had left some information for her and she needed to talk to him about the deadline for her work. She knew that she really needed to get back to it, but with everything going on for the last few days, she couldn't sit still long enough to write. She had decided that she would lock herself up in the house and get as much of it done as she could while he was gone. She didn't lack much, and maybe she could get it finished while he was gone. Most of it would just be transcribing the written pages to typewritten. She had hand written quite a bit of the book sitting in Tristan's hospital room while he was in the coma. So many sleepless nights, wondering what was going to happen. She bowed her head and said a silent prayer thanking God for the gift of their lives together.

Dan answered his phone on the second ring. The voice at the other end of the phone was Penny's. "I found your business car in my door, is there something I can do for you. Your wife was in the store last week and was admiring some silver pieces. Is she still interested in them?" She asked.

"It isn't about my wife and antiques, Penny; I need to talk to you about Danielle Bellefonte's diary. There is an entry in it that you and I need to talk about. Where can I meet you? Everyone in town knows about the diary and if I am seen talking to anyone, everybody just assumes that whomever I am talking to is either mentioned in the diary or is a suspect."

She thought for a minute and then said, "I need to go to the cemetery and put some flowers on my grandmother's grave. I can meet you out there in about thirty minutes." She said.

"Fine," he replied. " I'll meet you at the office. It should be far enough away from the actual crime scene to keep anyone from being nosey and the private parking in the rear should give us enough privacy."

Dan was waiting for her when she arrived. They exchanged greetings and sat down on a bench in the small garden just inside the private entrance. For the next little while he told her of the entry in the diary. The more he talked, the more she gasped for air. He told her some things that Danielle had written in the diary. After he finished telling her what had been written about her, he paused as if to give her a chance to speak. She said nothing for a long time. She got up and walked around to the other side of the table and sat facing him.

"Can I see this diary?" she asked.

"No, not yet. I have it hidden; no actually I am having it examined by an authority on the residents of this town. He should be deciphering it about now and giving me his advice. There are some pretty prominent people mentioned in there, Penny, and I am not really sure how to handle it. I am about this close to calling the federal authorities and turning the investigation over to them. Do you have any first hand knowledge of any of her "friends?" he asked.

"I know that she mentioned some names, but they were only brought up when we talked about the parties she attended. "Penny said. "Is any of this information I am about to give you going to be publicized?" she asked.

"No," he said. " All of it will be kept in the strictest of confidence. But I will have to tell you that anything that you tell me can be used in a court of law as evidence against you. Do you want to call your attorney?" He asked.

"No," she replied. "I don't have anything to hide. The only thing I'm going to tell you is this, I didn't kill her, and don't have the slightest idea who could have. Like I told you earlier, she and I went to a party one night and we both got pretty smashed.

We made it back to my house, had a few more drinks, and she got really drunk. I told her to stay over and sleep on the couch, as I was afraid she would hurt herself or someone else. I took some covers to the couch and made her a bed for the night. I retired to my room and fell asleep in my bed. Sometime during the night she woke up, came in to my bedroom, and got into the bed with me. I really didn't think too much about it at the time because my old sofa isn't the most comfortable place in the world to sit, much less try to sleep on. I didn't say anything to her until she turned over to me, put her hand up under my shirt and made a pass at me. I pushed her away and sat up on the side of the bed. She knew I didn't go for any foolishness like that. She told me that she had wanted to sleep with me for a long time, but never had the guts to tell me. I had heard that she was bisexual, but never saw her with another woman in any kind of intimate surroundings. Anyway, we had a pretty heated discussion and after a little while, she stormed out of the house and drove off like a mad woman. I swear Lieutenant; it is like I told you before when we talked in your office, I never had anything to do with her. We went to parties together, met for social gatherings, but shortly after that incident, she got drunk or high on something and called and taunted me about her sleeping with my ex husband. He had an unusual birthmark on a part of his body that no one usually gets to see. When she started describing that to me, I knew she was telling the truth. I knew she was trash, but tried to be friends with her because not many people liked her. I told her not to ever call me again and we only spoke when we were in public. That is the honest truth." She said.

"What did you think when you had heard that she had been killed?" He asked.

"I was just a shocked as everyone else was, I knew there were several people in town who didn't like her, but I didn't think that anyone hated her bad enough to kill her." She said.

"Have you seen any strange people in town lately or anything out of the ordinary?" he asked.

"No." she replied. "Everything has been pretty much the same since Julia Deveraux got back. You know she got involved with the soldier and what all happened there, don't you?"

"No," he replied. "Do you think I need to talk to him about this?"

"I don't think so, he was in the hospital in Jacksonville for a while and he is recuperating here. I think he has to go to Virginia for a few days, but he should be returning soon. He has asked Julia to marry him and I think that he just may become a permanent fixture around here. I need to tell you this, and I don't know if it means anything or not, but the District Attorney General, Alexander Graham, is Danielle's father. She told me that one night when she was drunk. She told me the whole story of the night she was supposedly violated and got pregnant. You might want to read the diary carefully; she sometimes put things in there that you have to read between the lines to decipher. Danielle was a really smart woman, she didn't act like it sometimes, but she was very smart."

He thanked her for her time and told her that he would call her and have her come in to make a formal statement if necessary.

"Damn," he thought. "This just gets more interesting every day."

As he was getting into his car, his cell phone rang; it was the judge.

"I think you need to come back to my office." He said. "There are a couple of incidents and people in here that we need to talk about. You may want to think more about calling in the federal authorities."

He closed the phone, and started the car. He sat there for a few moments and tried to process all of the information he had just gotten. Now he knew why the D A was so interested in the diary. He was wondering if he had been mentioned in it.

Dan *wondered* what the judge found? It must be something very interesting.

He didn't wait to be announced; he just walked past the receptionist and into the judge's office. He sat behind his desk with his back to him still reading the book. Dan pulled up a chair across from him and just as he sat down the judge turned around.

"Do you know who Danielle's father is?" He asked.

"Yes, but I just found out. Is he named in the book?"

"Yes indirectly, but it talks about him. They didn't get along at all. They had one hell of a fight a couple of weeks ago. He threatened to take her car away and she said if he did, she would tell his wife who she was. Apparently Mrs. Graham didn't know about the girl, and he definitely didn't want her telling his wife right now. Seems like they haven't been getting along very well, and this isn't really something that he would want broadcasted all over the world, either. They sat there for a while going over some pretty interesting entries. Many parties were listed, all types of meetings late in the evening, early in the morning. Conversations she had with her ex husband; a duke's mixture of information. But the most damaging was the argument with her father.

"Well, when are you going to show him this?' the judge asked.

"I am not sure that I am going to show him anything. I am going to sit down and talk to him, but you can bet your ass that I am NOT giving him the diary. He can issue all of the subpoenas he wants to, he'll never get his hand on this outside of the courtroom." Dan said. "I need to put this in the vault at the office, and make sure that no one else gets to it. I guess I need to see the old grouch pretty soon, the longer we drag this out, the longer it will take."

"Be careful," the judge said. "You could be walking on some pretty shaky ground. If the governor ever gets wind of this, he will have a field day with it. You know how they hate each other."

"Thanks for the help," Dan said. "I'll let you know how it all comes out."

"Just one question, Dan, what are you going to do if you find out he is involved?" the judge asked.

"Lock his ass up, I guess."

Tristan kicked his walking shoes off on the front porch. The smooth hardwood floors felt good to his bare feet. The smell of fresh baked cookies filled the air as he closed the door. As she walked into the room, he said, "You are quite the talented one, aren't you?"

"Not a bad cook either, huh?" she answered as she gave him a big hug.

As she pressed close to him she could feel the wetness of his perspiration on his shirt. For some reason this made her uncontrollably excited. She gave him a long kiss and ran her fingers through his hair. She helped him pull off his tee shirt and leaned closer. "There is something so enticing in the natural smell of a man." She said.

"You know I am going to miss you while you are gone, don't you?"

"Probably," he answered, "but think of how nice it will be when I get back. I shouldn't have to make any more long trips."

"How long will you be gone?" she asked.

"I'm not sure, but I am taking enough clothes for a week, hopefully just a few days; besides, I am going to have to go shopping for some civilian clothes when I get back. Know someone who might help me make the choices?"

"Maybe, now take your butt upstairs and get a shower, lunch will be ready soon." She said. With that he turned and headed towards the stairs. She spanked him on the rear and went to the kitchen to finish the sandwiches. She had just made a homemade chicken salad; her grandmother's favorite recipe. She prepared the small table on the back porch. The breeze was just cool enough to be enjoyable. Although the sun had already gone over to the other side of the house, you could still see the rays stealing their way through the branches on the trees. The sound of the ocean hitting the beach could just barely be heard. He leaned over and kissed her on the forehead.

"Why is it that I don't get that special lemonade any more? It has been a while since we have had it." He asked.

"It is for special occasions," she said. "I 'll try to make a batch for you and have it ready when you get back."

"I'll have to wait that long?"

"Of course, it is for special occasions, don't you remember me telling you that some time ago?" She laughed.

They enjoyed the lunch with out much conversation. There seemed to be something on his mind, and she was almost afraid to ask what it was. After he finished his sandwich, he asked," Do you like children?"

"Wow," she said, "that is not really what I was expecting, but yes as a matter of fact I do. I would like to have a dozen, but if I did I wouldn't have time for anything else. To tell you the truth it has been a long time since I had even thought about having children. What about you?" she asked.

"I have often wondered what it would be like to have a child. I am getting towards middle age and if we had one this year, which I am most sure we won't, I would be retirement age before they would be grown and out of the house. Something to think about. Just thought I would pick your brain." He said. He picked up the dishes and headed towards the kitchen. She followed him into the kitchen and as he was putting them into the dishwasher, she leaned against the counter.

"Were you really serious about us getting married?" she asked.

"Yes", he said. "I haven't been more serious about anything in my life. I would do it tomorrow on the beach if you would like, why?"

"I have been thinking, and I'll have to tell you that it scares the hell out of me, but I think I am ready for it. Do you think we should set a date?' she asked.

He walked over to the counter, ran his fingers through her hair, and kissed her softly on the lips.

"Let's see, today is the 17th of the month, how about the 21st?"

"Are you kidding?" she asked. "That doesn't give me much time to plan anything."

"Are you wanting a big wedding, or just what would you like to have?" he asked.

"I really don't know." she replied. "I have been thinking about this lately, and I think that whatever we do, I would like to go ahead and get it done. I know it is just a license and a commitment, but the thought of being Mrs. Tristan Broward just excites me to no end."

"OK then," he said. "While I am gone, make some preliminary plans, and we will finalize everything when I return. If you want to do it the next day, just make sure my tux, uniform, or whatever you want me to wear is clean and pressed, and we will get on with it."

She tried to hold back the tears, but just couldn't. He looked deeply into her eyes, and simply said, "I love you, Julia and I always will. Nothing makes me any happier than to be here, or anywhere else with you. I would be satisfied with a simple wedding on the beach, or you an invite one thousand guests, just let me know so I can make plans for our escape when the ceremonies are over."

With that he picked her up and carried her upstairs. He laid her gently on the edge of the bed. As he slowly helped her remove her clothes, he simply said. "The thought of having children excites me, but the thought of the practice in making them excites me more right now. Besides, I have to leave tomorrow and I need to practice as much as I can. I won't want to forget how to do this while I am gone."

"Me neither" she said. "I hope you never forget."

They spent the rest of the afternoon and night upstairs. You would of thought he was going to be gone for a long time. Every time she thought about him leaving, thoughts of the last time ran through her mind. Just before she went to sleep, she prayed for his safe return.

The drive to the airport the next morning was a pleasant one. He promised to call as soon as he got there, and she promised to make plans for the wedding while he was gone. As the plane took off, she couldn't help but remember the last time. She was sad that he was leaving, but the good thing was that when he returned, he wouldn't have to leave again; or at least she hoped he wouldn't.

Chapter Nine

Dan was in his office earlier than usual. He had the diary and was photocopying some of the pages. He figured that he could show the entries to Alexander if he denied any involvement. He had put the meeting off as long as he could; there was no getting around the confrontation.

He walked through the front doors and headed for the elevator. Although no one would be there for about an hour or so, he knew the old man would be in his office. He usually got there around 6:30 a.m. and never left before dark, no matter what time of the year it was. He entered the District Attorney's office and the reception area seemed eerily empty. There wasn't the faint smell of coffee as usual. Alexander Graham was the only person Dan knew of that drank more coffee than he did. He couldn't remember a time when he didn't see him with a cup of coffee in his hand. Once he had tried to take a cup in the courtroom with him, but the judge wasn't having any of that. Of course it just pissed the DA off even more, and the judge seemed to delight in that. As he walked down the hall, he had thought about going through the private entrance he had used the last time they had met, but the door had been locked and at the time he didn't really think anything of it. He knocked on Alexander's office door and there was no response. He tried the handle and as he opened the door, he saw something that he wasn't expecting. There he sat, one of the most powerful men in the state of Georgia. He had gone up against the governor several times, and had won most of the arguments, tried all of the major cases in the last twenty or so years, and won most of them also; but not anymore. There was a small handgun lying on the floor beside his chair, and there was a small trickle of blood from the entry wound in the side of his head. He had apparently committed suicide. Dan felt of his wrist for a pulse, but to no avail. He was dead, and from the looks of the place he had done it sometime overnight. It wasn't unusual for him to be there working most of the night. He hated to go home. He and his wife fought most of the time, and when they weren't arguing, she just wasn't talking to him. On his desk were two envelopes. One was addressed to his wife, and the other to Dan. "Dammit," he said under his breath. He expected a big argument with the DA, but never anything like this. He called his office from his cell phone and got the forensic officers on the way over there. It wouldn't be very long before the office workers would be coming to work and then it would be a fiasco. A few minutes later a couple of detectives arrived and started cordoning off the area. Dan let the photographer take pictures of the envelopes and then placed them in plastic evidence bags and held on to them. It wasn't long before the secretary came in. They had stopped her at the main entrance and when they realized who she was, they let her through. Dan met her at the office door, and gave her the grim news. "When was the last time you talked to him?" he asked.

"Yesterday afternoon when I left for the day." She replied. "He asked me to make sure that some of his cases had been updated and told me that he was going to be working late tonight and to please inform the security guards. I didn't really think much about it; he worked here a lot at night. I asked him if he wanted me to order anything for dinner for him, and he simply said no." Dan asked if he had been acting strange, and she told him that she had noticed something different about him for the last two weeks. She had overheard a heated telephone conversation he had with someone she didn't know, and was pretty mad when he hung up. When she explained the time frame of the telephone call, Dan realized that it was about the time that Danielle had been found murdered. The coroner's office picked up the body and took it down the service elevator to the morgue. An autopsy would be performed, but there was no doubt what the cause of death was. Dan tried to call Alexander's wife at home, but there was no answer. He asked the secretary if she had any idea how to get in touch with her, and she said that she hadn't talked to her in a few days, and just assumed that she had been out of town. Dan left and told the patrol officers to keep everyone out of the office. There would be a guard on duty all day. As he drove out to the DA's house, he tried to put all of this in perspective. The DA lived in an affluent part of town, although he didn't get to use the amenities of the subdivision very much. When Dan tried the front door to the residence, he found it locked. He walked around to the rear of the house, and noticed that Alexander's wife's car was parked in the garage. He made his way around to the back of the house and tried the door. It too was locked. Fearing that something had happened to her also, he broke the window and unlocked the door from the inside. About this time the maid pulled into the driveway and just as Dan entered the back door, she unlocked the front and walked in. After a few questions, he found out that Mrs. Graham had gone to visit her sister, and had been gone for about two days. Dan asked if there was a telephone number where she could be reached and Maria told him that she thought so, and would get it for him. When he finally got her on the phone, he told her she needed to come home quickly that there had been an emergency involving her husband, and she was needed right away. She replied, " I am not coming home, I hope the bastard dies! I had him served with divorce papers the day before yesterday, and I plan to stay a few days here in New York."

"I am sorry to tell you that your husband is dead, Mrs. Graham." He told her.

"He apparently shot himself sometime last night and the wound was fatal."

"Did he leave a note?" she asked.

"He left an envelope that was addressed to you. I have it in custody and it will be filed as evidence from he scene. I haven't opened it, but I will have to."

She told him that she would be on the next flight out. She apologized for the nasty remark, and told him that she and Alexander had been having some marital problems for quite a while and that she was tired of living with him. She had filed for a divorce and had the papers served on him at work. Dan told her that he would wait till she got back to open up the envelope, but that it would have to be examined because it was a part of the investigation. He questioned the maid about the last few days' events at the residence, and she pretty much had the same story that Mrs. Graham had just told him.

When he finally got to his office, he sat there looking at the envelope with his name on it. He wondered if he should open it alone, or should he call the judge and see what he thought. After a quick phone call, he opened the letter. It simply said:

To Lieutenant Dan Storey

Chief of Detectives

Savannah Police Department

If you are reading this then you have discovered my remains in my office. Two days ago my wife served me with divorce papers. A couple of weeks ago I had a very bad argument with my illegitimate daughter, and the day after that I found out that I had terminal cancer. The information on my daughter's death was really more than I could take. She wasn't the most liked person in town, and I know that her behavior needed some fine-tuning, however, she was still my daughter. I wasn't aware that she kept a journal until the day you visited my office. I was afraid that she would have written something like this in her book and that the information would expose me as her father. As far as I know you are the only other person outside of she and myself that knew this. After her death I told my wife about her and she didn't like it at all. I figured she should know from me instead of finding out from some outsider. I did not tell her about my illness, I wanted to wait to tell her at a later date; not wanting to spring two articles of this type of bad news on her in one day. After she told me that she wanted a divorce, I felt that it was a moot point to tell her. I would *appreciate it very much if you wouldn't divulge this information to anyone. I know that I am not very well liked in this county, but there are some things that are just better left alone. The knowledge of my past isn't going to be beneficial to anyone at this point in time, and it will just serve to embarrass my wife even more. One thing that I will tell you is this...... **I did not kill my daughter**. I have no idea who could have done such a dastardly thing. I know it was wrong, but I did give her money and a few other things when she called me. I thought it might keep her from telling the truth, but as I look back now, I should have just let her do whatever she thought was the best thing for her to do. There is a will in my lockbox at the local bank. My personal attorney has the instructions to open the lock box and read the will three days after my funeral. I have penned a letter to my wife and have told her everything she would need to know about both instances. The letter to her is of a personal note, and would not benefit you in any way to read it. Spare us all the embarrassment and leave the personal information in the letter to her.*

What you do with this information is of your own choice.

Alexander Graham
District Attorney General
Jackson County, Georgia

Judge Robinson took off his glasses and rubbed his temples. Dan had walked over to the judge's office and showed him the letter. He needed some professional personal advice.

"Have you shown this to anyone else?" he asked Dan.

"No, I really haven't had time, and besides, it really isn't any one else's business. What do you think I should do with it?"

"Well, if it was me, I would put it in a safe deposit box somewhere for future reference. I never would have thought the old bastard would have done it this way, but I guess it is better than waiting for the big C to kill him. Have you talked to his wife, and did you read the letter he wrote to her?"

"No, I have it, but I am not sure that it would benefit anything if I did read it. What do you think?" he asked.

"I would give it to her and tell her that you need to read it to make sure it doesn't have any information in it that would be pertinent to the case. You can do that, or open it now, read it for informational purposes, and then give it to her. It is your call. Personally I would leave no stone unturned." The judge replied.

Dan took out the letter and opened it in front of the judge. He stepped out onto the porch and read the letter. There wasn't anything pertinent to the suicide, or Danielle's murder; it was just full of information to Mrs. Graham in regards to her husband's banking affairs, his stock and bonds, and a private savings account he had kept from her for the last twenty five years. This is where the money came from that he had been giving to Danielle. There was a balance of over three hundred thousand dollars in it. The beneficiary was made out to her, and that she could do with it as she wished. He also informed her that the will would be read three days after the funeral, just in case she may have wanted to leave town for any length of time. He folded the letter up, and put it back into the envelope. When he walked back into the chambers, he thanked his friend, and told him that the contents of the letter had no bearing on any of the deaths; other than to just give his wife some financial information. The judge smiled at him, and said,

"I am glad you did that. I think it will keep you from wondering in the future what this was all about. Now you can get back to the matter at hand; solving the murder."

Dan walked out the door and headed back to his office. What a week, one murder, one suicide, and what will happen next? **"*These last seven days have been a bitch,*"** he thought. Maybe something will give, and he could get all of this closed out. What more could happen? Driving past Forsyth Park, his mind was a thousand miles away. He didn't notice the young man replacing the brick at the bottom of the fountain, nor could he hear what the young man was saying to himself;

"I have got to get this letter opener hidden. No one will ever think of looking here, nor will they ever know that I did it. Being the part-time keeper of the historical artifacts in these parks has afforded me the opportunity to dispose of this without anyone knowing about it. Maybe someday I can go to the police and tell them the whole story. Wonder if they will believe me when I tell them that I really did love her and that it was only in a fit of rage that it happened? Anyway, it will be safe here until I can get the courage to tell someone. I really wish I had stayed in New York where I belong. Coming down here was one of the worst mistakes I have ever made. I should have left her alone in the grocery store. I should have known hat she was too rich for someone like me. I am sorry that I ever met her. But, she shouldn't have embarrassed me like that. I was good enough to sleep with in the middle of the day when she wanted me, or when no one else was around, but not good enough to be seen out with in public. Here I am a graduate of law from Columbia University, and guilty of murder myself."

Jason Williams, newest addition to the district attorneys staff in Jackson County Georgia, graduated in the top five of his class, member of the track team, left the park in a hurry. Running down the sidewalk he cut between two parked cars, and didn't see the tour bus. Looking out of the side window of the bus, describing the parks to the tourists, the driver didn't see him until it was too late. Dan Storey's grandmother always said that deaths came in threes; looks like she was right again.

Back at his office, Dan was trying to piece all of this together. He could understand the suicide, hell; he wouldn't want to live with the idea of knowing that he could die anytime. Everyone he had been in contact with that had cancer had suffered miserably. As he was thumbing through the evidence, one of the detectives came in and asked if he had heard the news.

"What news are you talking about?" he asked.

"Another death from the DA's office. The newest addition to the staff ran out from between two parked cars and was hit by a tour bus. Apparently he never knew what hit him." How strange was this, two deaths in the same day from the district Attorney's office? He wondered if they could be connected somehow.

"Where is the body?" Dan asked.

"Still at the hospital, I assume. They had just pronounced him dead at the scene and are awaiting notification of next of kin. Apparently he was from up north somewhere and had no relatives down here."

Dan left his office and headed towards the hospital. As he entered the emergency room, the charge nurse asked if he wanted to see the body. After answering her he said, "Please get in touch with the coroner's office, I want an autopsy performed on him."

He drove to the scene of the accident and the immediate area was still cordoned off. He walked around the site for quite a while. No lunch bag, no drink containers, nothing that would make him think that he was having lunch there. What could he have been doing there? He lived several blocks away on the other side of town, and really had no reason to be there unless he was just exercising. Maybe the coroner could turn up something.

Number three for the week, "thanks Granny."

Chapter Ten

The officer's quarters at Langley were comparable to a new Holiday Inn. Not too many frills, but better than Motel 6. The first day of his debriefings had been hectic. They had asked all of the questions he had anticipated and then some. He found out that a terrorist organization had taken responsibility for the attack on the helicopter. Three days after the explosion killing all of his team members their deaths were avenged. The camp the terrorists had in the desert was already under surveillance for some threats they had made earlier. It wasn't hard for the Apache's to take out the whole camp. They should have been eliminated sooner, but the authorities had no idea they were going to be this big of a threat. As Tristan suspected, he was the only survivor. There was to be a ceremony at headquarters in a couple of days remembering them and giving them the Congressional Medal of Honor. The official report read that they were on a reconnaissance mission and were attacked maliciously. There was no mention of the retaliation in the report; it was just left up to the commanding officers to close the investigation. After dinner he settled down to read the complete report. After a short while, he called Julia to check on her. She missed him terribly and tempted him a little by telling him that she had just gotten out of the shower and was lying across the bed upstairs with no clothes on.

"You really know how to hurt a guy, don't you?" he said.

"No," she answered, "just want you to hurry home. In case you are tempted to go off on another extended vacation."

"Not a chance" he replied. "The next vacation I take will be with you."

They talked for about an hour and after explaining to her what would be happening for the next few days, he hung up the telephone. She put on one of his shirts and sat down at the old antique desk with her laptop. She had been working feverishly for the last few days trying to get her latest book finished. She was getting close to her deadline, and wanted to complete it on time. She loved her work, but like most authors, wanted to get it finished so she could start on some other ideas she had gotten in the last few weeks. She had finally come up with a title for the work, as that had been one of the biggest hurdles.

She had talked to Penny earlier in the evening, but there had been no word from Jared. She had asked Tristan if he knew anything, and he just simply said that he hadn't heard. Of course he knew that Jared had been sent on another assignment but didn't have any of the particulars. He wouldn't have told her anyway. Penny had told Julia that it had been quite a while since she had heard from him. "Maybe he is just busy," Julia said. " He may not be in a position to call or contact you."

"Yes, I know, but it would be good to hear from him."

Little did she know that he was on a slow moving ship somewhere in the middle of the Indian Ocean.

The commanding officer had offered Tristan an opportunity to form another team, but he declined. They talked for about two hours longer. Tristan told him that he was ready to retire. He had been around the world several times, and at this point in his life, didn't want to start up a new team. He had been assured that he would be reunited with Jared, but that was all that he could offer. They also offered him an administrative position but he declined it too. He took a picture of himself and Julia out of his briefcase and showed it to the commander.

"This is the main reason I want to retire. She is the most wonderful woman I have ever met. I just want to spend some time with her. We are engaged and although we haven't set a date yet, we will be married soon. I am ready. It has taken me a long time to meet someone this special and I don't intend to screw it up by possibly getting hurt like I just did. Besides, I don't think I could stand the thought of losing another team; we were together for a long time. I think it is just time for someone else to take over."

"I understand," the commander said. "I can respect your decision. I probably would do the same thing myself under these circumstances. I'll prepare the necessary paperwork, and have it sent to you. It will give you all of the instructions you need. You have served your country well. If you should ever decide to change your mind, don't hesitate to give me a call, personally."

As he left the commanders office, he thought of all of the many places he had been. He had visited most every continent in the world. There had been some beautiful sights, but none nearly as beautiful as Julia was to him. He wouldn't trade her for anything, and he couldn't wait to get back to her.

CHAPTER ELEVEN

Dan walked into the coffee shop and went immediately for the large cup dispenser. Yesterday had been one of the most trying days of his career. The forensic report was to be ready this morning from the young man whom had gotten killed in the traffic accident yesterday. He wouldn't have been so interested in it but two deaths from the District Attorney's office in one day was troubling him. He filled his cup and walked out the door. He savored the taste of coffee in the mornings. His wife detested the smell of fresh coffee, much less the taste of it. She was a cola person, day or night, it didn't matter; she liked the cola taste as much as he did the coffee taste. When he walked into his office, the report was not on his desk. He called the coroner's office and got the person in charge of the investigation. He was in the process of preparing the autopsy and forensic report.

"Did you find anything unusual?" Dan asked.

"No DNA evidence," the examiner said. "There were some fresh cement particles under his fingernails. You don't usually find stuff like this under the fingernails of people who work in offices; and the strange thing about it was that it was only under the nails on his right hand."

"Now why would he have cement particles under his fingernails?" Dan wondered. He thought for a minute longer, and walked out of the door. He returned to the scene of the accident trying to retrace the steps of the young man. He walked down the sidewalk into the park. He had thought that he had seen the young man once before, but couldn't place him. It had finally came to him that he had seen him the first day he had been to see Alexander about the diary. He had passed him in the hallway. The young man had walked hurriedly past him with his head down as if he was hiding something or was ashamed to look anyone in the eye. But what had he been doing before he was hit by the bus? As he sat down on the park bench to finish his coffee he got a phone call from the officer that was investigating the accident. "Did you know that the deceased worked part time for the parks department?" he asked.

No," Dan replied. "But what does that have to do with anything? He could cut grass, sweep the streets, or just clean the statues. Most young attorneys don't make a lot of money and they have to do something else to help with the drain on their checking accounts to satisfy their lifestyles. Did anything turn up at his apartment?"

"No sir, just a receipt for some roses he had bought."

"Do you know who they were for? Maybe he was seeing some married woman and her husband was chasing him or something when he ran in front of the bus. Who knows?"

Things were getting a little out of hand. He couldn't figure out why he couldn't get this off his mind. He wasn't much on relying on gut feelings, but his gut was telling him that there was something amiss with this.

"No sir," the officer replied. "His place was immaculate. Everything was in place and clean as a pin. That is except for his briefcase."

"What was wrong with the briefcase?" Dan asked.

"It had a hammer and chisel in it. Looks like he had been doing some brick work with it. The residue on the chisel was still kind of damp, as if he had just finished working on something." He said.

"Bring it in with you, I want to run it through the lab to see if there is some resemblance to the cement particles that were under his fingernails. Be sure to put it in an evidence bag so none of the material will be lost." He said.

Dan called the lab and talked to the technician whom had done the initial autopsy on the body. He told him to analyze the particles from the briefcase and compare them to the substance that was found under the victim's fingernails. As he sat there on the bench he racked his brain over the events of the last few days. Could there be any connection between the young lawyer and Danielle? None of her neighbors had seen anyone coming or going except the one time, but most of them weren't up in the wee hours of the morning when she would come home either. No one had gotten a license number from the lexus, and there were too many black ones in town to search that angle very much. He went back to his office and made a list of the people that were involved in this case; both directly and indirectly. He called Penny and Julia to ask if they had known the young lawyer or if they had any knowledge of Danielle knowing him. They both said no. Penny hadn't spoken to her in quite some time, and Julia was just an acquaintance of hers and really didn't know much about her personal life.

As he hung up the phone the technician walked into his office. He dropped two microscopic photographs on Dan's desk.

"The particles from the briefcase are the same material I found under his fingernails. Whatever he did, he was doing just before he ran out in front of the bus. Judging from the apartment he lived in, the way he dressed, and the condition of his office, he was a very clean person. It would be out of character for him to have dirty fingernails, especially dirty with cement and sand particles. He had been digging something out or putting something back together would be my guess. It may not be too far from where he was killed either. He was on his lunch break, and although he had a part time job for the park services, why would he be doing something in a business suit? Strange isn't it?"

Dan thanked him for the information. He went back to the park and retraced the victim's steps again. When he got to the statue in the middle of the park he examined it closely. None of the bricks looked like they had been disturbed; that is until he got around to the base on the backside. There he noticed that two of the bricks looked like they had fresh mortar around them. As he examined them more closely, he saw that the mortar had a different color than the rest. He called the forensic team and had them come back to the park. He also had the detectives assigned to the case to come back out and block the area off. As the technicians began digging around the bricks, they came out without much trouble. When they removed them from the base there was something inside the base of the statue; wrapped in a cloth. Dan took the bundle and laid it on the ground. As he opened it, there appeared to be bloodstains on the cloth. As the cloth unfolded there was a handkerchief wrapped around a metal object. A closer examination of the contents revealed a silver letter opener. The handkerchief that it was wrapped in bore the initials D.B.

"Take this to the lab and compare the blood on the cloth to the samples we took at the crime scene for Danielle Bellefonte." Dan told the technician.

"I'll be damned," he muttered under his breath. It has got to be. The initials on the handkerchief matched hers, and the letter opener was about the size of the wounds in her chest. How could he be so lucky? This had to be one of the toughest cases he had ever been involved in. He had to caution himself to not rush to conclusions, the blood still had to match. Maybe there would be some fingerprints on the letter opener. He wasn't counting on it though, if he had wiped the car clean enough to not leave any evidence, then he doubted if there would be any on the weapon. Dan called Penny Oglethorpe and asked her to come down to the station. He showed her a picture of the young lawyer, and asked if she had seen him before. She replied that he had been in her shop a couple of times, looking for "presents" for his mother. Although he hadn't bought anything, he looked in her shop for a long time. He then showed her a picture of the letter opener. "Where did you get that?" she asked.

"Do you recognize it?" Dan asked.

"I sure do, it was stolen from my shop a couple of weeks ago. I have been looking for it everywhere."

"Could it have come up missing about the time he visited your shop?"

Penny thought for a little while and then she agreed that it had come up missing shortly after the young man had been in her store.

"We got two matching fingerprints off it and they belonged to him. The blood on the shank matched the sample from Danielle's body. It appears that he is the one who stabbed her to death and left her in the cemetery. Do you know anything about him?" he asked.

"No," she replied.

"I never saw them together and she never mentioned him when we talked. Of course I would not have heard about him if they met after we had our differences. We didn't have any civil conversations after the incident in the grocery store. Is there any connection to the suicide of the Attorney General?"

"Not that I can find out, but that is another reason that I brought you in. Penny, no one else knows about his relation to Danielle but a choice few. Meaning myself, you, Mrs. Graham, Danielle and of course Alexander. There is no need for anyone else to know about it either. I am asking you for your help in this matter. Graham was dying of cancer and Mrs. Graham had filed for a divorce. He told her about Danielle after he was diagnosed and she couldn't deal with it. That is when she filed for the divorce; after he told her about Danielle. He never told her about the cancer. There is very little mention about it in the diary and I would like to keep it that way. There is no need for the scandal to get all over the newspapers and circulate through the local gossips."

"What are you going to do with the diary?" Penny asked.

"I think I am just going to destroy it. There are some pretty damaging accusations in there, and there are also some entries about some late evening meetings with some prominent people in this town. I think some things are just better left alone, don't you?

I mean, there is mention of you and her having lesbian love affairs. Do you want that all over town? I don't think so." He replied.

"You are right, there is no need to say anything about this to anyone else. " she said.

"As far as I am concerned, the information should go no further, and you can lock that letter opener up in your vault somewhere and forget it is there. I have no use for it ever again. As bad as I disliked her, I couldn't bear having it in my shop again."

With that she stood up, shook his hand, and walked out the door.

❧

The door to the judge's chambers was shut and Dan asked if his honor was busy.

"Not really sir, he is just out on the porch smoking as usual. Go on in." she said.

He stopped by the judge's desk and took one of the cigars out of the humidor. His honor was sitting on the porch smoking and looking out over the city. Dan sat down, lit the cigar, took a big puff and loosened his tie.

"I have some bourbon in the bottom drawer if you would like. Sounds like you need a little shot."

"No thank you," Dan said. I just need a little time to digest everything before I close the case. I guess you heard what happened."

"Yes, but you need to clue me in on the real story, I have only heard the scuttlebutt."

The judge remarked.

Dan spent the next two hours going over the scenario of things that had happened in the last couple of days.

"Isn't it amazing how you can run into a dead end and all of a sudden the road opens up?" Dan said.

"You never know what is going to happen." The judge replied. "But you know, most of the time it all comes out in the wash, doesn't it? By the way, what are you going to do with the book?" he asked.

"Don't really know." Dan said. "It is evidence, but I cannot afford to let it fall into just anyone's hands. There is some pretty incriminating information in there, and it would cause a lot of problems for some pretty important people in this town. I think I will just seal it and put it in the vault with the letter opener and close the case. It is clearly a crime of passion and there is no need in hurting anyone else. The DA took the easy way out, he was dying anyway, and he just hastened it so he wouldn't suffer. If the bus hadn't hit the kid, I would still be out there trying to find out who did it and it would haunt me for the rest of my life."

"Sounds like a good idea to me," the judge said.

Dan crushed out the butt of the cigar and stood up. As he turned to go back inside he took two handwritten pages out of his coat pocket. "I thought you might want to read these. After you read them, I suggest you burn them or run them through the shredder. They are the only ones that were torn out of the diary. Your secret is safe with me."

Judge Robinson took the pages and opened them up. A few minutes later he took out his lighter and set them on fire and let them burn to ashes in the ashtray that he kept on the outside table. He watched Dan walk across the street again. Dan was right; some things were better just left alone.

CHAPTER TWELVE

Tristan got off the plane to the cool evening air. There she stood; the most beautiful woman in the world. When he got to the gate she came running out to meet him. She kissed him for a long time.

"Welcome home my darling," she said.

"It is sure enough good to be home, and to know that I will be staying for a long time. Have you set the date yet?" he asked.

She was somewhat taken aback with his question, but answered no, that she had been thinking about it but wanted to finish her manuscript before she started making final wedding plans.

" I want to do it as soon as possible. I have been thinking about it for a long time, Julia, and I don't want to put it off any longer than we have to." He said.

"How about tomorrow on the beach?" she asked.

"OK, if you can get it together by then." He laughed. They talked all the way home. They would be married in two weeks on the beach on Tybee Island. It would be a small ceremony with Penny as the maid of honor and a best man of Tristan's choice. He had tried to contact Jared, but had no luck. There were no living relatives that could come down and participate, so they just nixed the idea and had it by themselves; just the two of them and the preacher. Penny stood behind the sand dunes and took pictures. They were married in the evening and the portraits came out beautiful. The sunset in the background was the most beautiful one she had ever seen. She called her agent and told him that the manuscript was ready. He would have plenty of time to read it while she was on her honeymoon. She would be enjoying the cruise and this time Tristan would really be on a vacation while at sea, with no fear of the enemy interrupting him this time.

Epilogue

Twenty years had passed since that glorious day on Tybee Island. Almost one year to the day that they had gotten married Julianne Deveraux Broward was born. She was a healthy little bundle of joy. Tristan and Julia had lived in the old home place since the day he came home from the hospital. After the honeymoon they had settled in and never left each other's side. They would take early morning walks, and evening strolls. Even when she was close to giving birth, she would still take the afternoon walks with him. The novel she wrote while he was in the hospital; "The Confederate Lovers" made the Wall Street Journal's best sellers list. She held four book signings that year, and it sold over a million copies. While she was giving birth to Julianne, they found out that she had a degenerative heart disease. The doctor said that she was lucky to make it through childbirth. She was very weak for a long time after Julianne was born. Eventually she got worse and just couldn't handle it any more. Just after Julianne's eighth birthday, she died in her sleep. She knew something was wrong, apparently, because she left Tristan a note. She lay there for a long time cherishing the way he held her as she always did. When he awoke the next morning she lay there almost angelic.

The note simply read:

My Darling Tristan:

We have spent many wonderful days together. The seven days we were together when we first met were the best of my life. I loved you from the beginning and grew to love you more each day. When Julianne was born and I saw those little blue eyes, I knew no matter what happened, you would be alive as long as she was. I cannot thank you enough or tell you how much I love you. Words could not describe the feeling I had when I was with you. Lying in your arms always made me invulnerable to the worries of the world. I have put a picture of me in the locket you gave me many years ago. Please give it to her whenever you feel the need. I am hoping that she will cherish it as much as I have. Please continue to take her to the lighthouse. She enjoys it just as much as I did when my mother took me out there while my father was gone. I have always loved you my darling, never forget that.

Your Julia.

The doctor had told them at the last visit that it wouldn't be much longer and wanted her to stay in the hospital or go to a medical facility where she could be cared for. Tristan wouldn't hear of it. He stayed by her side the whole time. He would carry her downstairs every morning and back to the bedroom every evening. Penny would come by every other day to check on them, and help with Julianne. After Julianne would go to bed, he would take out the note and read it. He loved Julia with all of his heart and he missed her every day.

As the years passed, he never remarried. He always was there for Julianne what ever she needed. Penny Oglethorpe had been a great friend. She kept the antique store open until she just couldn't stand to be around there anymore. After Julianne's sixteenth birthday," Aunt Penny" decided that it was time that she saw the world. She sold the antique shop and booked a cruise. While on it she met a professor from Virginia and six months later they were married in a small ceremony on the front porch of his family's old plantation estate. She never heard from Jared again. She kept in touch with Tristan via mail, and even introduced her new husband to him when they visited Savannah once. Tristan tried to find out what happened to Jared, but every time he got close to an answer, he would run into a dead end. Tristan walked to the mailbox one day and there was a small package there. There was no return address on it, but you could tell that it had traveled a great distance. There was a note inside that simply read:

Dear Lieutenant Broward:

My dad always said that if something happened to him to send this to you. He said you would know what to do with it. He spoke of you often, and though it was hard for him to get around after his injury, he still relished the memories of the times you two had together. I would hope to be able to meet you someday; he spoke very highly of you.

Good luck and god speed.

Jared, Jr.

He opened the box and there was a medal that Jared had been given on their third mission together. He stuck it in his pocket and when he got inside; he walked up the stairs and added it to his collection.

Julianne had met a nice young man from Mobile, and had been married for about seven years. Tristan's grandson liked to play with the old "buttons" that grandpa kept in the little wooden box. On her 21st birthday, Tristan took Julianne into the attic and got out the old jewelry box that held the seashell locket he had given her mother on their second date. He told her the story of the note and asked if she wanted to read it. He said that it would be hers whenever she wanted it. She read it and simply told him no, to keep it for as long as he lived. She knew what it meant to him. Tristan only visited Julia's favorite breakfast restaurant once after she died. He had walked the beach many times, but just couldn't bring himself to go back in there. The one time he did go inside, he sat at their favorite table for a long time. He could see the smile on her face from the last time, and the embarrassment in her smile, as she would sign the front pages of the books of the patrons who always wanted her to autograph them. There were copies of each one of her books displayed at the counter, with a picture of her standing on the back porch of the cottage.

He visited Bonaventure Cemetery every week and put fresh flowers on her grave. He finally had to get rid of the old Chevy. It had been a monument to her from day one. As for the old Ford in the basement; some time after Julia's death Tristan restored it and drove it around town some. He had a license plate made for the front that bore her name. When Julianne graduated from college he gave it to her for a graduation present.

Judge Robinson sat the bench for a total of twenty-five years. His cigar smoking finally got the best of him and he died of emphysema. Dan tried to get him to stop even after he had quit himself, but he never would. A few days after the judge's death, Dan took Danielle's journal out of the evidence room and carried it to the beach. He lit a small fire and watched the pages burn to nothing. Penny had long since moved away, and as far as he knew, he was the only person left in the world that knew the contents. She had kept her word and never said anything to anyone about the information in the journal.

Daniel Storey still visited the coffee shop every morning even after he had retired. There had been many murder cases in his career, but never another one like the Danielle Bellefonte case. Sometimes he and Tristan would cross paths as Tristan stopped in the coffee shop some himself. They even had talked a couple of times when they were in there together, but neither realized that in their lifetime, they both had a remarkable "Seven Days in Savannah."

JW AMBROSE

www.ingramcontent.com/pod-product-compliance
Lightning Source LLC
Chambersburg PA
CBHW020038310726
48970CB00007B/2304